# THE WOLF CONSORT

RITE WORLD 5: RITE OF THE WARLOCK

JULIANA HAYGERT

# COPYRIGHT

# AUTHOR'S NOTE

I hope you enjoy reading *The Wolf Consort!*

Don't forget to sign up for my Newsletter to find out about new releases, cover reveals, giveaways, and more!

If you want to see exclusive teasers, help me decide on covers, read excerpts, talk about books, etc, join my reader group on Facebook: Juliana's Club!

# RITE WORLD

Welcome to the RITE WORLD!

The Vampire Heir (Book 1)
The Witch Queen (Book 2)
The Immortal Vow (Book 3)
The Warlock Lord (Book 4)
The Wolf Consort (Book 5)
The Crystal Rose (Book 6)
The Wolf Forsaken (Book 7)
The Fae Bound (Book 8)
The Blood Pact (Book 9)

# 1

THE LAST THING I REMEMBERED WAS LEAVING DARK WITCH Manor with Wyatt. The next thing I knew, I was being half-dragged down a long, cold corridor.

I closed my eyes, fighting against the fuzziness clouding my mind. What was going on?

Two men tugged my arms and threw me inside a room. I tripped on my feet and fell on my knees, my legs jarring from the impact with the rough, cold stone.

I blinked and focused just long enough to see the two men retreat and close the thick, wooden door—a door with a small cutout on the top and metal bars.

Panic filled me as my mind cleared, and I finally remembered what had happened. As Wyatt and I were skirting the mountain and avoiding Dark Witch Manor and Bonecrown territory, someone attacked us.

We had blacked out.

And now, we were in some kind of damp, cold medieval dungeon with gray stone walls and almost no light.

I scooted to the door. "Wyatt?" I called, worried about

him. I hadn't seen him since before blacking out. What if they had killed him? What if they had left him behind? "Wyatt, can you hear me?" I didn't shout; Wyatt would be able to hear me whisper, depending on his state. This way, I could avoid our captors' wrath. "Wyatt?"

A low growl came from the other side of the door.

I took a lungful of air and let it out slowly, trying to shoo the grogginess away. My sight cleared a bit and when I pulled up, holding on to the door, I didn't feel like I was going to puke.

I spied out through the small hole on the door. Cables ran through the low ceiling and a few naked lamps hung from them, illuminating little of the wide corridor of gray stones lined with doors like the one I was hanging from. Without a doubt, I knew Wyatt was behind the door across the corridor. But what state was he in?

"Luana?" he asked, his voice low.

"Yes! How are you feeling?"

"I'm fine," he mumbled. "A little dizzy and sleepy, but not hurt. At least, I don't think I am."

"Do you know where we are?" I asked, hoping he had stayed awake long enough to see the faces of our captors. "Who attacked us and brought us here?"

"No," he whispered. "I passed out half a second after you did, I think. I only woke up when I was thrown in here a couple of minutes ago." He grumbled again, probably still too affected by the attack.

What had they done to us? And moon be cursed, who were they?

I shook my head.

This couldn't be happening. No, this was a nightmare.

Wyatt and I had been with Keeran and Farrah at Dark

Witch Manor. We had helped Keeran defeat Soren, his evil warlock father. The warlock had fled. We had been there when Zell, one of the rebel warlocks, asked Keeran to assume the role of warlock lord and lead the warlocks. Keeran had accepted the title.

And, it hadn't even been forty-eight hours since I had found out Keeran was my mate—after an amazing kiss that almost led to more. Fortunately, Keeran hadn't noticed the mating bond snapping into place, and when I pulled back, he thought I was still mad at him for lying and rejecting me.

If only it were that simple.

And now I was locked in a dungeon, only the moon knew where.

It did sound like a nightmare.

The sound of footsteps reached my ears and I straightened, trying to get a better look through the small opening, but it was only when the man was right in front of the door that I could see him well.

I sucked in a sharp breath. "Soren."

"Hello, Luana." He smiled at me, his lips stretching and showing off his ridiculously white teeth. He looked like a creep. "I'm so glad to see you again."

Fury filled my veins, sending the rest of my stupor and dizziness away. "Moon be damned, what's going on?"

"What do you mean?" He looked around, as if searching for something. "What's wrong with your accommodations? Don't you like my new place?"

That caught my attention. After all, I wanted to find out where exactly we were. "New place?"

"Where are my manners? Luana, welcome to the Chateau of the Cursed."

I frowned. "Another named place?"

"Oh, I have dozens," he said, as if he had said he had dozens of shirts or shoes. "All around the world. Just in case."

In case of what? He was defeated and had to flee? Convenient. I pushed against the door. "What do you want with me?"

He tilted his head. "I thought you would have figured that part out by now." What was he talking about? "You're the most important person to Keeran. When word gets to him that I have you, he'll come for you, and I'll kill him."

My stomach dropped.

No, Keeran wouldn't be that stupid. But maybe he would. If it were him locked in here and Isalia was trying to lure me in, I wouldn't think twice. I would face Isalia to get to Keeran. No questions asked.

I suspected he would do the same for me.

"No," I whispered.

In the other cell, Wyatt groaned.

"Oh, and that pup of yours," Soren said, glancing at the wooden door at his back. "He has no value to me. I'll be disposing of him."

I slapped my hands on the door. "You—!"

"Ah, ah." A thin, cold grin appeared on his lips. "Watch what you say. You're in my house and I can be a bad host if you press me. Just try me and you'll see."

"You piece of shit!" I yelled, not caring about his threats. To lure Keeran here, Soren would have to keep me alive. But that didn't mean he had to keep Wyatt alive. With one contemptuous last glance, Soren spun around and marched away. "Come back here!" I called, though I knew it was fruitless.

The adrenaline of facing Soren faded away, leaving my muscles sore and my entire body tired. My skull screamed where they had struck me. My back against the heavy door, I slid down to the cold floor.

What now? I couldn't stay here and wait until Keeran came to rescue Wyatt and me. But what could I do locked in this cell?

By the moon, Keeran would come and face his father to save me.

Was Keeran ready for that?

I wished we didn't have to find out so soon.

The light from the lamps outside flickered, bathing my cell in darkness. When the lights came back on, I noticed something in the corner of my cell.

My bag. They had thrown my duffel bag in here too. I crawled to it, wishing I had packed a big ass weapon, so I could break out of here. But there was nothing useful inside. Otherwise, I doubted they would let me have it.

There were only clothes and the crystal rose.

Hands shaking, I took the crystal rose and stared at its beauty. In the dim light of the cell, the rose shone as if there was a light coming from inside. I cradled it against my chest, and my brain turned to Keeran again.

I don't think he realized what this flower would mean to me when he gave it to me. To him, it was probably something he picked up and made prettier. To me, it meant he had thought of me. That he cared enough about me to make this beautiful thing for me.

And how did I repay him for it? By getting captured.

If only there was a way I could get out of here.

In my hands, the rose's red glow intensified. I held it out and stared at it as the rose color shone brighter and brighter. What was going on?

A faint red smoke snaked out of the rose and floated in

the air, traveling across the cell. It wrapped around the lock. A loud clicking sound rang. The red smoke faded, and the rose lost its glow.

I held my breath.

Could it be?

Slowly, I made my way to the door. With a trembling hand, I reached for the lock and pulled. The door swung open.

What the ...

I didn't allow myself to stop and think. I jumped up and raced across the corridor. "Wyatt," I called. "Get ready. We're leaving."

"W-what?" he mumbled.

"We'll have to fight our way out."

I wrapped my fingers around the rose and willed it to work whatever magic it possessed. It had unlocked my cell door; it had to do it again for Wyatt's door. But as much as I stared at it, the rose didn't shine.

"Luana?" Wyatt asked.

"Give me a second." Tears sprang to my eyes. No, no, it had to work again. "Come on," I hissed.

But nothing happened.

I was so lost in my attempt to create magic, I didn't even hear the footsteps or catch a whiff of their scents until they were in the hallway.

"What do you think you're doing?" a warlock shouted.

I started to shift.

"Not this time," another one said. He threw a black bolt at me.

It hit me squared in the chest, knocking me down and taking my breath way. Pain coursed through my back, and it only got worse as I was dragged inside the cell again.

One of them picked up the rose from the floor. "What is this?"

No! I must have dropped it when I was hit. I snarled. "Give that back to me!"

"I don't think so." The warlock pocketed the rose.

Another one closed the door of my cell with a finite click.

"No!" I fought against the pain, the dizziness, the surprise, and raced to the door.

"Make sure you cast some spells on the lock," one warlock said. "She can't escape again."

I saw the shine of the black magic hitting the lock as the warlock reinforced my door.

Nevertheless, I pushed against it again.

Their chuckles rang clear through the corridor as they walked away.

A tear rolled down my cheek.

By the moon, I had almost escaped. Somehow, I had managed to make it outside my cell.

And now I was locked in again.

I doubted I would have another opportunity like that again.

## 2

KEERAN

I STARED AT THE THRONE AND IT STARED BACK AT ME.

The fancy black chair made of thick twisted branches with a black velvet cushion now possessed my name, but for some reason, I couldn't sit in it.

It had been a couple of days since Soren, my father, had run away and I had accepted the title of warlock lord. Since then, a lot had happened. Luana and Wyatt had left, and Farrah had remained here in the castle to help out, though most of the warlocks were wary of her—I knew how that felt. The servants and the witches were gone. The remaining warlocks, about three dozen, also helped in cleaning up the mansion, reorganizing classes, and distributing tasks. Now that the servants and maids were gone, each of them would have more to do around here.

So far, everything was going smoothly.

The only thing still bothering me was Luana. She had left with Wyatt a little over two days ago. She should have reached the Dark Vale pack already. Shouldn't I have received a message from her by now? I would give her one more day and then—

"Just sit on the thing already," Farrah said, snatching my attention. She was seated on the steps before the throne, and she looked at her long nails as if there was something important hidden in them. "It won't bite, you know."

No, it wouldn't, but the moment I sat on it, then it would all become real. Too real. I didn't want to admit it, but I thought that once I sat on the throne, the weight of my title would hit me full force and drag me down.

Instead of replying to Farrah, I talked about something else. "So? Are you still bored?"

She had been complaining about being bored since Wyatt and Luana left. I knew she felt something for Wyatt, even if she hadn't said anything, and now that he was gone, she probably felt lost.

Just like I felt a little lost without Luana here with me, helping me, supporting me.

Farrah shrugged, flipping her long silver hair back. "I've done all I could for you." That was true. She had helped a lot while we freed the prisoners and cleaned up the castle, but once the planning of the warlocks' everyday life began, she had no input. "I want to go. I just need to figure out where."

I had asked about her brother and her realm, but she hadn't said much. For some reason, she didn't want to share anything significant about herself. I suspected she was afraid of getting hurt. Or being pushed away. Kicked out. Banished, just like her group had done to her.

"You know you can stay here, right?" I had told her that a dozen times already.

"And I already told you. One fae among a bunch of warlocks? Not my thing."

I chuckled.

"My lord." I cringed at Zell's voice. I still hadn't gotten used to that freaking title. I spun around and found the warlock marching toward me. His gray eyes were serious, and his long light brown hair was tied behind his back. "It's time for your lesson."

I nodded. "Right."

Because of my unstable magic, Zell had taken upon himself to teach me more and help me get a handle on my powers. In between all the chores, we met twice a day to practice.

Without a word, we went outside, to the back garden, where it would be less likely I could hurt anyone.

In the middle of the garden and under the baking sun, Zell and I faced each other.

"Let's begin," he said. "Channel your magic."

The few lessons we had always began the same way. He instructed me to channel my magic and hold it in for a brief moment before performing some kind of spell.

I took in a deep breath and called my power. It answered instantly, filling my veins with pure energy. "Done."

"This time, we'll do things a little different," Zell said. "Instead of holding it for a few seconds before letting it go, I want you to let your magic grow inside you, to the point where it seems like every inch of your body will explode. Then, you'll hit a target."

He waved his hand and the trunk of a short tree at the edge of the garden smoothed, becoming a flat board. Red circles like target zones appeared in the middle of the smoothed trunk.

"Let it out bit by bit, sending weak bolts, while keeping

control of the power inside you. Keep going until the magic is almost all gone."

I frowned. Not sure I liked this idea. Last time I tried a similar exercise where I channeled all of my power and held it inside me, I almost killed that cursed witch Giselle and her two friends.

This time was different though. I didn't hate Zell or want to hurt him. Also, Zell would be ready. If something went wrong, he would use his magic to fix it.

I let out a long breath. "Okay. I'm ready."

Closing my eyes, I called more of my magic. It answered fast and filled my veins even faster. I kept channeling more, as Zell had instructed, until it felt like I would suffocate. Magic took up every available inch in my body.

"Now, let it out." Zell pointed to the target. "One small hit at a time. Go."

Bracing myself, I raised my hand, palm out, and aimed for the target. I gritted my teeth and sent a ray of magic out. The small relief was short lived, and I quickly sent another two hits, just to reduce the pressure inside me.

The first strikes hit the target, but the other two were a big miss.

"Shit," I muttered, trying to regain control over my power.

"Try again," Zell said.

I shook my head once and sent another weak ray at the target. It hit right in the middle, adding another dark burn mark to the wood. But like before, it wasn't enough, and before I knew it, I let out another three hits.

Still, the pressure didn't let up. Instead, it felt like it kept growing, as if I hadn't stopped channeling my power.

I fought against it, but my power escaped me.

A big red ray flew from my hands and hit the tree. It

exploded on the wooden trunk, showering us with small wooden pellets and burned leaves.

"Holy shit." I stared at the dead tree. "I'll never get this."

Zell sighed, but didn't seem affected otherwise. "Don't say that. You will get it. You just need more time."

"But Luana will need us soon," I said, hoping it was true. "I don't have much time."

"Unfortunately, controlling magic isn't as easy to learn as it seems," Zell said. "The other warlocks and I were born in amid this. We always knew about our powers and we grew up practicing them. Even if in the beginning we had trouble controlling our magic, we practiced and eventually got the hang of it. But you didn't have that luxury. You're like a kid trying to learn how to ride a bike, but as an adult. It'll be harder for you, but that's why you have to practice more. Harder." He swept his hand and a tree a few feet from the first one became our new target. "Again."

I opened my mouth to tell him my temper was rising, which would only make my control over my magic more unstable, when Flavius, an older warlock who had been handling more of the new organization inside Dark Witch Manor, walked into the gardens.

"My lord, you have a visitor," he said.

I frowned. Who could it be? "Bring him to the throne room. I'll be right there."

Flavius bowed his head before disappearing inside the manor.

"You seem rather relieved by this interruption," Zell teased.

I offered him a small grin. "I could use the break before I lose my temper."

"I see." Zell gestured to the castle. "Please, my lord, go see your visitor. I'll find you later for another practice session."

"And here I was, hoping you would let me take the rest of the day off."

Zell snorted. "No, my lord, I won't go that easy on you." He bowed again, then marched away, heading to another wing of the house.

I went back to the throne room.

I skidded to a stop when I saw the tall fae with long silver hair and dark blue eyes a few feet from Farrah, who seemed to have every muscle of her body coiled and ready to attack.

That was a surprise.

"Daleigh," I called out, a little wary. Last time I had seen Farrah's brother, he had tried to kill us. I walked up to Farrah and stood by her side. "What brings you here?"

"I come in peace," he said, shifting his gaze to me. "I'm sorry I asked to see you, warlock lord, but I thought that was the only way I would be allowed in here. The truth is, I'm here to talk to my sister."

Farrah stiffened. "We went back to your camp about a week ago and it was destroyed. Soren's warlocks confessed that they attacked you, but they wouldn't tell us what happened exactly. I searched the forest nearby and didn't find you. What happened?"

Daleigh nodded. "They attacked us, and even though we had to flee, nobody was seriously hurt. I'm sorry to have worried you."

"Then ... what do you want?" she asked.

"I need your help," he said, as if he hadn't banished her.

Farrah crossed her arms. "I can't see why."

"There's another fae group." Farrah's violet-blue eyes

widened. Daleigh went on. "I tried to make peace with them, but there is too much bad blood. Our courts have been at war for so long that they won't listen to me. They've been attacking us."

"Wait? Is this nearby?" I asked.

Daleigh cut me with his cold eyes. "Yes, but it doesn't concern you or any other supernatural race." He returned his gaze to Farrah. "This is about the fae."

"And why do you want my help?"

"Because you're the most powerful of us all," he said. What did he mean? I had seen Farrah's magic before, but I hadn't thought much of it. Was she really the most powerful fae? "You can help me end this dispute before it becomes a war and claims the lives of many innocent fae."

"What do I get in return for helping you?" Farrah asked.

Surprised by her words, I turned to her. "You aren't seriously considering this, are you?"

She let out a long sigh. "I was just complaining I was bored, wasn't I?"

"You'll be welcomed back. No questions asked," Daleigh said.

But I had many questions. What the hell happened in the first place that made him kick her out? And why was this so important that he was now willing to welcome her back?

"Farrah," I called, not sure why I was feeling so riled up in her stead.

"Okay," she whispered. "I'll go."

I stared at her.

Daleigh's shoulders relaxed. "Thank you."

Farrah turned to me. "Thank you for everything you've done for me, Keeran."

I blinked, still taken aback. "You're leaving? Right now?"

She nodded. "I'm needed. At least for a while."

"Wait ..." This was too fast, too sudden, too weird.

"We should go," Daleigh said. "We have scouts in the area. They will be back soon with intel. We'll use that to either attack or defend, and I would like to be there for that."

"Right." Farrah smiled at me. "Goodbye, Keeran."

Daleigh glanced at me. "Until we meet again, warlock lord."

And just like that, the two of them walked out of the throne room.

For a long while, I stood there, as if nailed to the floor, barely breathing.

I felt like I had been completely abandoned. First, Luana and Wyatt, and now Farrah. If I wasn't in a castle full of warlocks, I would feel as if I was lost again.

I cleared my throat. "Flavius? Are you out there?"

The warlock marched inside the throne room and bowed. "Yes, my lord?"

"Is there any news about Luana and Wyatt?"

"No, we haven't received any message from them yet."

"Thanks," I muttered.

I spun and faced the throne at the end of the room.

It stared back at me.

I would give Luana another day. If she hadn't sent word by then, even a quick message, I would surrender to the worry gnawing at my gut.

Who was I kidding? I was already sick to my stomach with worry.

She better be safe, or I would kill her myself for being so stubborn.

# 3

LUANA

After three or four days locked in the cell, I lost track of time. There were no windows, so I didn't even know if it was night or day.

I could have been here, cold and weak and starving, for a week, or six months, or a year. I had no idea anymore.

I didn't know what time it was when a couple of warlocks entered my cell, and after binding me with magic, dragged me out. A few moments later, I was taken past a large archway and into a wide room with a high ceiling and gray walls. I was thrown on the cold, dark floor in front of two long dining tables.

A moment later, Wyatt was shoved down beside me.

"L-Luana," he mumbled, looking at me. I hadn't seen him since the day we left Dark Witch Manor and had been attacked, though we checked on each other by talking every couple of hours. He looked terrible. His face was thin, pale, dark circles crested beneath his eyes, and bruises covered his arms. I bet I didn't look much better. "What's going on?"

"I don't ..."

My words died as I looked up at the table closest to us. Soren sat at the end of the table, a satisfied smile on his lips. "Welcome to dinner," he said, his voice loud and chipper. "Well, my dinner. And you're my entertainment."

I tried making sense of his words. "W-what?"

A moment later, a human with a purple eye and a busted lip, limped to the table, carrying a big silver tray. She deposited a goblet of wine and a plate with a small portion of food in front of Soren.

"Your appetizer, my lord." Her voice trembled almost as much as her hands.

With her head low, the human woman retreated, and Soren gestured toward us. "Begin."

The four warlocks who had brought us here stepped closer, their eyes shining with eagerness. A chill ran down my spine as I realized what Soren meant by entertainment.

Torture.

Wyatt and I would be tortured.

The magic binding my arms behind my back tightened, and an invisible grip grasped my throat. Helpless and gasping for air, I jerked against nothing. I couldn't see anything and I couldn't fight it. The magic around my throat tugged me up, and I scrambled to my feet. It kept pulling me up until I was on tiptoes.

"Luana!" Wyatt shouted. He lunged toward me, but magic enveloped him and within seconds he was in the same position I was.

Soren pointed his finger at me. A black ray hit me in the chest. I screamed as pain filled my rib cage, twisted my gut, and burned my veins. It radiated from my heart to my arms, down my legs, to my toes.

I gasped against the grip around my neck. I jerked against

the hold on my wrists. I kicked my legs, trying to find a better position. But nothing helped.

Then Soren sent another black ray. This time, the pain was deeper and spread slower. My senses blurred.

Dark spots filled my sight. My muscles didn't obey me anymore.

By the time the third ray of magic struck me, I couldn't even scream. I shook with pain, and once it raced down my body and was gone, I sagged against the grip on my neck.

I was going to suffocate, but I didn't have any strength left to fight.

The sounds of banging and yelling reached my ears, and I tried to process what was happening. It took me a moment to realize I wasn't dreaming or having a nightmare.

A dozen wolves burst into the dining room, jumping the warlocks and taking them down. The remaining retreated to one side of the room, from where they sent spells at the wolves, keeping them away.

I fought against the pain and dizziness and stood on my tiptoes again. The hold on my throat lessened, but it was enough for a slow breath. My vision cleared a bit, but my senses were shot. Who were these wolves? Although I couldn't help but hope, I doubted they had come to save Wyatt and me.

Soren shot from his chair and retreated to the corner with his warlocks. Focused on the battle, he let go of his magic around my neck, and I fell to the ground like a big potato sack.

Wyatt scooted closer to me. "Are you okay?"

I groaned, trying to break the binding around my wrist, but that magic still held strong. I opened my mouth to tell him this was our chance to run, when one of the wolves shifted.

The battle stopped and the warlocks gawked as the wolf took the form of a beautiful, naked woman.

I gasped. "Isalia …" I had been so out of it, I hadn't recognized her in wolf form.

She stood tall in front of the warlocks, completely unaffected by the way they ogled her. "Luana is my wolf. She belongs to my pack. Hand her over to me so I can finish her off."

Soren scoffed. "What makes you think I'll give her to you?"

She put her hands around her waist. "Because if you don't, my wolves will attack and rip your warlocks apart."

With slow steps, Soren approached Isalia. His eyes roamed over her body. "You're quite beautiful."

She shrugged. "What does it matter?"

Soren walked a circled around her. "I'll give you Luana on one condition."

"Which is?"

Soren stopped in front of her and extended his hand to her. "Make an alliance with me. Join me." She narrowed her eyes. "I can sense your power. You're a strong alpha. Together, you and I can do incredible things. Powerful things. We can rule the world." He smiled at her. "Together."

Behind Isalia, the wolves snarled, as if they didn't like this idea.

I expected Isalia to laugh in his face, then attack him. Instead, she slipped her hand in his. "I like that idea."

My jaw fell open.

"This can't be happening," Wyatt muttered.

Soren brought her hand to his lips. "Now, for your gift." He stepped to the side and gestured to me.

Shocked by what had happened, I had missed my window to escape unnoticed. But I could try now. I scooted back, trying to find something to help me get to my feet, so I could run, but before I got far, two warlocks hooked their hands under my arms, pulling me up.

"Luana!" Wyatt shouted.

I jerked against their grip. All they did was use magic to tighten their grip on me.

They brought me to Isalia.

By the moon ...

She smiled at me. "Dear pup, I missed you." Her eyes locked on my cheek and went down to my neck. "What a nasty scar. It completely ruins your pretty face."

A growl built in my throat. "You gave it to me, bitch."

Isalia let out a loud chuckle. "Oh, I know, and that's why I enjoy it so much." She glanced at Soren. "Drop the magic on her. I want a fight before I kill her."

A fight? Every inch of my body hurt, my head swam, and my vision still had plenty of dark spots. It wouldn't be a real or a fair fight, but I had learned nothing was fair with Isalia.

Soren moved his hand and the magic around my wrists dropped. Too hurt and exhausted from the damn torture, I wobbled and fell to my knees again.

Instantly, Isalia shifted.

Shit.

Through my dizziness, I called my wolf.

But before I could complete the change, smoke exploded from the main door and filled the room like a dense fog. Warlocks and werewolves coughed.

Me too. And the more I tried to breathe through it, the

worst it was. I coughed more and my head spun, as if I had been hit with magic again. I blinked but all I saw was a dark gray wall, as if I suddenly had gone blind.

There was something magical about this fog.

I struggled against it, but I could feel my strength slipping out.

"Wyatt," I called. He let out a low groan from somewhere to my side. I crawled toward him.

Then a hand covered my mouth, and another pressed around the back of my neck. "You're okay," a voice said. "You're okay now. Sleep."

I jerked, trying to get rid of the person holding me, trying to push away the dizziness, fighting the magic making me groggy.

But my muscles felt leaden, and I was sinking into a dark ocean.

I blacked out.

# 4

I HADN'T SLEEP WELL SINCE LUANA HAD LEFT, AND TONIGHT was no different. I tossed and turned in my bed. I closed my eyes and thought of good things. I focused on the fact that I was in a fancy room, on a freaking soft bed, even softer comforter, in a protected mansion ... what else did I need to relax and rest?

And yet, sleep evaded me.

I remained in bed for as long as I could endure, but it was just past five in the morning when I couldn't take it anymore. I knew what was wrong with me. It wasn't just because Luana wasn't here, but also because another three days had passed and she still hadn't sent word to me.

Something had to be wrong. I didn't like it, but that was the only explanation I had. Otherwise, why was she so quiet? I had waited longer than I had first promised myself. Enough was enough.

I shot up, got dressed in black leather attire, and went down to the main office on the first floor. At this time of the morning, most of the warlocks were still sleeping, and the place was eerily quiet.

However, near the office's door, a young warlock on patrol bowed his head before resuming his march through the manor.

"Galroth, wait," I called.

He turned to me. "Yes, my lord?"

"I have a task for you."

"What is it?"

"After you finish your patrol, rest for a couple of hours, then leave to find Luana and Wyatt," I told him. "I want to know what happened and why they haven't sent me a message yet."

Galroth lowered his head. "Yes, my lord."

"Thank you," I whispered.

He marched away, and I walked into the dark office. This had been my father's office, from where he planned the destruction of all witches and the other supernaturals. In the past few days, I had found creepy journals and dark magic books that I wanted to destroy. Instead, I locked them away, in case he ever attacked us again and I needed a weapon against him.

I knew Soren wasn't done with me.

Because of that damn prophecy.

During my free time the past few days, I had gone through the extensive library on the other side of the castle and searched for anything I could on prophecies. So far, I hadn't found anything useful, but I still had many books to look through.

Letting out a long sigh, I made my way to the library and resumed my search from the spot I had stopped the last time. Slowly, I walked among the tall wooden shelves, running my finger down the spines of each book. If the title seemed like it could contain anything about prophecies, I plucked the book from the shelf. Once I had ten books in my hands, I sat down on one of the long tables in the middle of the library, and skimmed through the books.

Almost an hour later, I had found only seven books, but soon everyone else in the manor would be up and my busy day would start. I took the seven books to the table and sat down.

"My lord?" Zell entered the library. He stared at the pile of books on the table in front of me. "What are you doing in here?"

I gestured to the tables. "Still looking for information on prophecies."

Zell pressed his lips together. "My lord ..."

I narrowed my eyes, suddenly thinking he was hiding something from me. "What is it?"

A long breath escaped Zell's lips as he took the seat across from the table and faced me. "Your mother, Acalla, was called the oracle because of her powers of prophecy. It was she who made the prophecy about you before you were born."

"W-what?" That didn't make sense. "If that's true, then she wouldn't have told Soren about the prophecy." Otherwise, she had willingly put a target on my back.

"She didn't want to tell him," Zell continued. "He found out."

"How?"

"Honestly, I don't know. But I know one thing ... Acalla was able to hide something about the prophecy from Soren."

"What do you mean?"

"There's another part of the prophecy only a few people know," he said, his eyes darkening. "You'll only be able to come into your full powers and become a true warlock after you kill your father." My gut twisted. "But once you do, you'll have to pay a price: your sanity and your goodness. You'll turn dark and mad like your father."

I shook my head, because nothing of what he said made sense. "It can't be."

"It's how it's supposed to be."

"Then I won't kill my father and I won't become mad and evil."

"It doesn't work that way," Zell said. "All of Acalla's prophecies have come true. They are inescapable. Which means, you will kill your father and you'll become evil."

I shook my head. "I won't accept that. Our fates aren't sealed. Prophecies can be changed. There has to be another way. I won't kill my father."

Zell's brows curled down. "Why is it so horrible to accept? Soren is an evil man. By killing him, you'll be saving the world."

"Didn't you just say I'll become evil like him? I'll save the world from him, but who will save the world from me?"

"We'll worry about that when the time comes," Zell said. "Right now, you must be willing to do whatever it takes to seize power from your father. You need to accept your fate." He paused. "You have to understand, the warlocks who have stayed hate Soren, but they don't want a weak warlock as their leader. Not all of them will follow you if you don't prove you're capable of doing what needs to be done. Otherwise, the others will try to overthrow you. You must prove your birthright by shedding blood."

I shot up and the chair fell back with my sudden movement. I stepped back. "I don't like this. I don't want this."

"Then you should prepare to hand over the leadership to a more capable warlock."

A warlock who wouldn't turn evil.

The idea wasn't appalling. However, for some reason, I didn't like having to step back and hand over something I had just received. First, Zell had convinced me I was the perfect warlock lord, that I could bring them into to a better world. And now he was telling me I was destined to become evil no matter what. How was that a better world?

Unless he had plans to kill me. But why didn't he just kill me now, then?

Confused, I shook my head. I had made up my mind. "I would rather give up my power and my title than become evil."

"I don't think you understand how this prophecy thing works." Slowly, Zell stood, his eyes downcast. "Even if we try to change it, even if you abandon your title and appoint someone else to become warlock lord right now, nothing will change. You don't have a choice. The prophecy will still happen. You'll kill your father, become the warlock lord again, and become evil."

# 5

My werewolf senses kicked in before I fully woke up and opened my eyes. Peanut and chamomile scent, the heat of fire, and in the distance, the sound of a waterfall.

I sat up and looked down at myself—I was wearing loose white pants and shirt, almost like a hospital gown. What in the moon? Curious, I glanced around. I was in a full bed in a small room. The window was closed, but the curtains were half-drawn, revealing the bright sun outside and the room's door was opened.

I closed my eyes for a moment and tried to remember what had happened. Soren had summoned Wyatt and me for a torture session while he had dinner, but the chateau was attacked by Isalia and her wolves. Soren and Isalia made an odd alliance, and Soren, instead of using me to lure Keeran, had given me as a gift to his new lover—ew! But as Isalia was about to kill me, a heavy fog covered the room, someone grabbed me, and I fainted.

And now I was in this unfamiliar house, completely lost.

However, the dizziness and the weakness were mostly gone.

Which meant, I could get up and find out what was going on—and escape if necessary.

Careful not to make a peep, I got out of the bed and tiptoed to the door. I spied into a short hallway. There were three doors and an archway, which led to what looked like the living room, and beyond that was the kitchen—or at least it seemed so because of the noise of the water boiling, the opening and shutting of cabinets doors and the fridge, and the short footsteps that moved from one side to the other.

Who could it be?

Slowly, I made my way into the living room and looked into the adjacent dining room, and beyond a tall counter, the kitchen.

A beautiful, tall woman, with long brown waves cascading down her back, stood in front of the range.

"I just rescued you from a bunch of warlocks and were-wolves," she said, her voice firm but with a soft edge. I stilled. "If I wanted to hurt you, I would have done it while you were unconscious. Or I could have left you there."

I took a couple more steps, but stopped on the other side of the dining table. "Who are you? What are you?"

With delicate movements, the woman picked up the screaming kettle from the range and filled up two teacups with hot water. She dropped the kettle and picked up the saucer from each teacup and turned.

She was even more beautiful than I first thought, and older too; she was probably in her early fifties. Her dark brown eyes were warm, and her smile seemed true enough. "Here." She placed the teacups on the counter. "I made some tea for you."

I frowned. "Did you know I was awake?"

"I knew you would wake up soon," she said. She grabbed the honey from the counter to the side and put a few drops in her cup. "To answer your questions, I'm Almae, a witch, and you're in my home."

"You rescued me. Why?"

She sipped from her tea. "I was there on a mission. It got sidetracked once I saw the battle and you being tortured and about to be killed. I couldn't stand for that."

I looked around, forcing my hearing far and wide. "And where's Wyatt? You rescued him too, right?"

She rested her teacup on the counter and looked down. "I tried, but a handful of werewolves were on top of him. There was nothing I could do."

Gasping, I took a step back. "You don't mean ..."

"I'm sorry," she whispered.

No, no, it couldn't be. Wyatt wasn't dead. He was too young, too lively to be dead. "I have to go back and rescue him."

With the second teacup in her hand, Almae approached me. She placed the teacup on the dining table and pushed a chair back. "Here." She reached for me and, holding my elbows, guided me down to the chair. She sat beside me. "I'm sorry, but there's nothing you can do. If you go back now, you won't find him, and you'll only be handing yourself to them on a silver platter."

The burn of tears made me blink fast. "No ..."

"He seemed like a loyal wolf. I'm sure he died content that he could help his alpha."

I wiped at my eyes, getting rid of my unshed tears. "I'm no alpha."

"Yes, you're the true alpha of the Dark Vale pack."

I frowned. "How do you know so much about me?"

She smiled. "I know a lot of things. For example, I know Isalia cheated and took the alpha title from you."

"But I cheated before her." I slapped my mouth, shocked I would confess such a thing to a stranger.

"That wasn't your doing," she said simply. "But you're right. Nevertheless, you cheated. That doesn't mean you're not the true alpha. You just didn't snatch the position the right way."

This woman was strange. She spoke as if she knew everything, as if she were wise, even wiser than Bagatha ever was. Bagatha had been the queen of all witches. Almae had said she was witch, but nothing else. "What is this place? What coven are you from?"

"No coven. We're in a hidden village," she said. "Tomorrow, when you're feeling better, I'll show you around."

I stood up, eager to find out more about this place. "I'm feeling better n—" A wave of dizziness hit me, and my muscles trembled. I fell back on the chair. How did she even know this?

"You should rest some more." She pushed the untouched teacup toward me. "Drink. I'll make supper soon and you should eat too. Only then you'll recover your strength and feel better."

She stood and strolled back to the kitchen.

My curiosity only increased with each passing second. A secret mission, a single witch, a hidden village, and more knowledge than necessary. I wanted to ask her a million questions, but as if she had cast a spell on me, I felt my head getting heavy, my shoulders sagging. I was too tired to even stand.

Giving in to the witch's suggestion, I drank the tea—it was a nice, sweet chamomile with a hint of vanilla. "I like it."

She glanced over her shoulder and smiled. "I'm glad. Oh." She dropped the pan she had grabbed and walked back to me. "I almost forgot." She reached inside the pocket of her skirt. "I found this with a warlock who was keeping guard." She fished the crystal rose from her pocket and offered it to me.

I stared at it, suddenly taken aback that she had recovered that from the warlocks. I didn't know why I cared so much about a damn rose. But I did.

Tears sprouted in my eyes as I wrapped my fingers around the crystal rose's stem and cradled it. "Thank you."

"There's powerful magic inside that rose. You should keep it safe."

I stared down at the rose. "It was a gift."

"I know. The rose was made to protect you. If you lose it, it won't be of any help, will it?" Keeran did that? He had imbued the crystal rose with magic to help me? "But there's a catch. It only helps you. If you use it to help others, it won't work."

So that was why it didn't unlock Wyatt's cell when I tried? Once more, this witch was shocking me. "Seriously, who are you?"

Almae waved her hand at me. "Just an old witch, trying to do the right thing." She turned her back to me and marched back to the kitchen. "Now, which do you prefer: zucchini casserole or chicken parmigiana?"

---

## 6

KEERAN

IT TOOK GALROTH ALMOST THIRTY-EIGHT HOURS, BUT HE CAME back and found me late at night in my father's old office. As usual, I couldn't sleep and preferred to try to do something productive instead. Like fretting over news that never came.

Until it did.

The moment Galroth stepped into the office, I shot up from the chair.

"So, what did you find?" I asked, my stomach tight with anticipation.

"Nothing," he said, his eyes serious. "I searched the entire area around Dark Witch Manor, I took the path down the mountain you mentioned, I checked around Bonecrown territory, and I even went to the Dark Vale pack, but there was nothing. No one."

"Wait." I hadn't heard him right. "Are you saying the Dark Vale village was deserted?"

"Yes, my lord. It's empty. As if the werewolves packed up the essentials and left."

That didn't make sense. The Dark Vale wolves had vanished? Luana and Wyatt were nowhere to be found?

Panic snaked through my chest, pressing against my rib cage and hurting. My breathing came out in little, rapid puffs. "Galroth, gather a team immediately. We're going to find Luana and Wyatt."

"That's unacceptable." Zell's voice rang from the door.

I turned hard eyes to him. "What did you say?"

Impassive and imposing, Zell strolled into the room. "With all due respect, running our coven and finding Soren and fulfilling your prophecy is more important than finding two wolves who left of their own accord."

My fists clenched as curses rose in my throat. How dare he say that of Luana and Wyatt? Rage coursed through my body, and it was all I could do not to attack him right then. "Zell, Galroth, as your warlock lord, I order you to get a party ready. We'll leave in an hour."

I met Zell and Galroth and ten warlocks in front of Dark Witch Manor.

Energy and anxiety filled my body and I could barely stand still.

"We'll patrol the area, searching for clues on Luana's and Wyatt's whereabouts." Even though most of them weren't formally introduced to the two werewolves, all the warlocks knew who they were. They knew Luana and Wyatt were my friends.

"What happens if we don't find anything?" Galroth asked.

"We'll go down the mountain and follow the path they were supposed to take," I said, my voice loud and clear.

Galroth and the warlocks exchanged a glance. Annoyance flittered in my gut. "Understood?"

"Yes, my lord," they answered.

I gestured to the path ahead. "Let's move out."

The warlocks began marching. I followed them, my mind trying to think of a spell, a more powerful tracking spell, but other than some random, silly enchantments, I couldn't remember anything.

I was too worried to focus, and I was afraid that would make me miss something vital.

Zell fell into step with me.

"My lord," he began. The superior tone in his voice made me grit my teeth. "As your loyal subject, I have to insist that this is not a good idea. With all due respect, please, my lord, think about this. The warlocks will get the wrong idea. Their leader doing all this for two werewolves? It's not the message you want to send out on your first week as the warlock lord."

"Those two werewolves are my friends." I clenched my fists, fighting the urge to punch him. "The message here is that we're good and help our friends."

"Those friends left as soon as the battle was finished. They barely helped cleaning up afterward."

The freaking bastard. I halted and loomed over him, hoping my stance was menacing enough. "They stayed. They helped. They ran around like crazy, doing all they could to help."

"But they left."

"Because they had to go back to their pack, which is also in chaos," I snapped. "And once I hear from them, we'll help them, just as they helped us."

"My lord—"

"Enough, Zell," I cut him off. "Either help and do what I ask, or go back to the manor."

Before my cursed temper exploded and I either punched him or shot some magic bolts at him, I marched off with fast, long strides. I didn't slow down until I was in front of the group.

I couldn't lead them through a search irritated like this. I would either snap at everything they said, or I would miss the clues I sought.

To calm down, I took in half a dozen slow breaths and imagined Luana smiling at me. My mind wanted to keep going and fantasize about her leaning into me, standing on her tiptoes, and then kissing me—my heartbeat sped up again for a totally different manner.

I shook my head once and channeled my magic, focusing. I forced my magic to give me better sight, so I could see any clues Galroth might have missed.

"Use your magic if you need to," I told the group. "Just find me something."

I felt as the air rippled when they called their power and used tracking spells and other tricks to find them.

After an hour patrolling the area, a heavy feeling settled in my chest. This wasn't right. How could they have disappeared? The only explanation was that they had either been abducted or killed. But by whom? Isalia wouldn't have been quiet about it, and Galroth hadn't mentioned finding her anywhere either. So Isalia was missing too?

Maybe it was my father and his warlocks? But he had fled, with his numbers cut down to a third. He wouldn't be ready to attack so soon, would he?

Right now, it didn't matter who did it, as long as we found

Luana and Wyatt and rescued them. Later, I would kill whoever had done this.

Another hour passed, and I started hearing chatter behind me about the warlocks being tired and hungry and lost.

Irritation began deep in my core, but I pushed it down. I called on my magic to mute their voices from my ears and to enhance my sight a little bit more.

There had to be something out there.

There had to be.

Walking in a big circle, we ended up crossing a rock formation, which resembled a huge bear again. And this time I saw it.

A drop of blood on the tip of a fallen leaf, mostly hidden by an arching bush, right beside the edge of the rock formation. I skidded to a stop and the warlocks followed my lead. Hands trembling, I picked up the leaf. It was freaking blood all right. I glanced around and saw a broken bush and a line of flattened grass, as if something heavy had been dragged through it.

"It's here," I called out, panic filling my chest. "They were attacked here and taken."

"My lord," Zell began. I braced myself, knowing I wouldn't like what he was going to say. "You have to consider that they are gone."

I frowned. "What do you mean?"

"If they were taken and there has been no contact, no ransom messages in more than a week, then you have to believe they weren't just taken. They were killed."

My gut dropped like a rock. My throat went dry. "No ..."

"There's nothing you can do for them now," he said. "We

should go back to the manor and focus on more important tasks."

I summoned my power without even noticing it. I pulled my arm back, ready to let it all out—

"My lord!" Flavius's voice cut through my rage-induced daze, and I turned to him. Flavius? Here? He hadn't come on this search. He ran to me. "A message arrived at the manor a little while ago." He held a folded white paper in his hands. "I was told it's urgent."

I stared at the paper. Could it be? The ransom note? Was that it?

Holding my breath, I picked up the paper and unfolded it.

*Meet me at Bagatha's old cottage.*
　　*Thea*

My brows slammed down. This wasn't what I was expecting. But ... Thea was a powerful witch. With her power and knowledge, I was sure she could cast the right spell and find Luana and Wyatt.

I crumpled the paper in my hand and looked out at the warlocks surrounding me. "Go back to the manor."

"What about you, my lord?" Galroth asked.

"I'll be back later," I answered, my voice cold. "I have something that needs my attention."

# 7

MY NIGHT HAD BEEN RIDDLED WITH NIGHTMARES. FIRST, Keeran and Soren were battling at Dark Witch Manor, and Soren killed Keeran. Then, Wyatt and I were taken by Isalia and forced to duel for days—each time she was about to win, she retreated, let me recover a bit, then attacked again. Later, I was back at the Chateau of the Cursed, where Soren tortured me with not only magic, but also ancient weapons.

Lastly, I saw Keeran walking into the Chateau of the Cursed to rescue me, but I was already dead. And he was tortured and killed.

Sweating, I sat up in bed and stared out the window. Behind the mountain, the first rays of sunlight tainted the dark blue sky with soft pinks and oranges. I focused on that beautiful view, because if I didn't, my mind conjured the images from my nightmares and I couldn't deal with those anymore. Not without getting sick or crying my heart out.

When the sun finally peeked from behind the mountain, I gathered my will and left the bed. I found a change of clothes on the nightstand with a note on top.

· · ·

*The bathroom is across the hall. There's a towel, soap, and hair products for you there.*

How did Almae know I was dying for a bath? Was that part of her magical knowledge too, or simply common sense? I was going with the latter here.

With slow movements, so I didn't get dizzy, I grabbed the clothes from the nightstand and went to the bathroom. It felt good to take a proper shower after who knew how long, to scrub myself clean, to wash my hair.

After the shower, I put on the black pants and beige shirt Almae had given me, I brushed my hair, and when I looked in the mirror, I felt more like myself than I had in a long time—despite the thin white scar marring my face and neck.

I averted my eyes.

How could I be so upset about a damn scar when Wyatt was dead? He was dead, and it was my fault. If I hadn't insisted we left Dark Witch Manor when I had, if I had told him to stay with Farrah, as I knew he wanted, if I had been able to unlock his door with the crystal rose, if I had protected him like a real alpha could ...

Tears brimmed in my eyes, and this time, I let them out.

The young wolf was dead, and I could do nothing to change that.

I let myself cry for a couple of minutes, then gathered myself. When I had the chance, I would perform a burial ritual for him, even if I had to bury air in his stead.

Like the day before, I found Almae in the kitchen, but

instead of making tea, she was bringing food to the table—lots of food.

"Good morning," she said, smiling at me. "Please, sit down and have breakfast with me."

I took a seat at the table, staring at all the warm bread, the pancakes, the bacon, the eggs ... "You made all of this for us?"

She sat down across the table from me. "I know you didn't sleep well, and with your werewolf metabolism, you're probably hungry." She pushed a wicker basket filled with muffins toward me. "Here. Dig in."

---

"READY?" ALMAE ASKED, HER HAND ON THE KNOB.

"Ready," I answered, feeling like a kid going to see the circus. After we ate, I helped Almae clean up, before she made good on her promise to show me the village.

The older woman opened the door and stepped out.

I squinted under the sun, but my wolf eyes adjusted and I looked around.

Her small cottage stood atop a hill. A narrow stone path, flanked by colorful flowers and fluffy bushes, reached her door and snaked down the hill, curving to different sides and reaching other cottages that dotted the hill. Down below was the base of the mountain I had seen earlier with a short waterfall, a deep lake, and what looked like a town square with stands and stores, like a marketplace. And walking around the square, talking and smiling and laughing, were many supernaturals—witches, werewolves, vampires. Were those warlocks? I even caught a glance of a fae or two.

"Are you just going to gawk, or do you want to check it out?"

I shifted my wide eyes to Almae. "What is this place?" I asked as we walked down the stone path.

"We call it Unity," she said, her voice proud. "For years, I've been working on a place where all supernaturals can coexist without being afraid of politics or coven or pack rules." She spread her arms wide. "It's a small, hidden place, and we only welcome those we deem worthy."

"Worthy? What do you mean?"

"I mean, those who have a good heart and have the same vision as us. Supernaturals who would rather enjoy life instead of living for battles and killing." She lost her smile. "Or hide from terrible pasts. Can you imagine what would happen if someone evil knew about this place? We would be decimated."

We reached the market, and as soon as we began our trek among the stands, the supernaturals bowed their heads to Almae. In turn, Almae smiled and greeted them all by their names.

"My queen," a few whispered as we walked by.

I frowned at Almae. "Queen? You're their queen?"

She flinched, but she didn't lose the amused, loving expression on her face. "It's just a title they gave me. I never intended to become a ruler, but I guess a community without guidance would become chaotic in no time. But I consider myself more like a president. I don't rule alone. I have advisors, a couple of each class, and we decide everything together."

Everything about this place amazed me. The way Almae described her ruling, the various kinds of supernaturals milling around the market and talking to each other like they were friends. Here, there was no power, no ego, no discord.

That, or I was being tricked like Keeran had been at Dark Witch Manor.

Suspicion grabbed hold of me fast and strong.

"What's wrong?" Almae asked as we veered toward the waterfall.

Despite all my doubts, I couldn't deny this place looked and felt like paradise.

"This sounds and looks too good to be true," I confessed. "I'm waiting for the other shoe to drop. At some point, I'm going to turn and see the vampires attacking the werewolves, or human slaves being tortured in the corners, or you cackling like a mad witch who ensnared the clueless wolf."

She laughed. "My word, you have quite the imagination."

I frowned. "It's not my imagination. I've seen it all before."

Almae's lips turned down. "I'm so sorry you have lived in such a terrible world."

I did, but I had had friends and people I cared about in that world. And I had been snatched away to this enchanted place. If this really was true, then I had found paradise.

"Why did you save me?" I asked, my voice low.

Almae halted a few feet from the lake and stared at the waterfall. "I told you I had gone there on a mission, didn't I?" I nodded. "I had this vision once that the world could be a better place, but despite all my effort and fighting, nothing changed. So, I created my own little corner of happiness. A hidden one, but real nonetheless. Nowadays, I don't get involved in anything outside of our walls, but when I learned Soren had been kicked out of Dark Witch Manor and was on the move, I knew I had to act."

"You know Soren?"

She dipped her chin once. "I went to the Chateau of the Cursed to kill him. Imagine my surprise when I found the place being attacked by a group of werewolves, and two of them being tortured."

"That still doesn't answer my question."

"I felt something in you." She shook her head once. "I saw something in you. I knew I had to save you, to keep you safe, because you have a better future ahead of you, if you follow the right path."

What ominous advice. "The right path? Most of the time I don't even know left from right." Which was a lie. I did know left from right, but I got caught up in the many shades of gray between good and evil.

She smiled at me. "Don't worry. You'll know what I mean soon enough."

I wanted to ask more, but something about Almae's rigid posture and raised chin made me swallow my words. I filed those questions away for another time.

I lifted my head, soaking in the warm sun. This place was beautiful, perfect. I wished Keeran could see it.

My heart skipped a beat.

Keeran. I had promised to contact him, to let him know when to come to aid me, and that was how many days ago? Four? Six? Eight? I had lost count ... I hoped he wasn't worried about me. He must have known I never intended to contact him.

But what if he was still waiting?

"Is there a way to send a quick message?"

Almae gave me a side glance. "To your mate?"

I stared at her. "H-how do you know?"

She shrugged. "I told you. I know many things."

"So you know he's a warlock and I'm a werewolf? The mating bond was drunk when it snapped into place."

She chuckled. "I know what he is, and I think the mating bond chose right. He's perfect for you."

"You talk as if you know him."

Her smile faded. "I know enough."

"Then you also know we can't be together. He's supposed to be the warlock lord, and if I go home, I'll fight to become alpha again." At this point, I wasn't sure what to do. Wyatt was gone, my pack was lost in Isalia's madness, and she had joined forces with Soren. I had no chance of defeating them. "My pack would never accept a warlock as their alpha's mate."

"It might be a challenge, but you can't deny your heart forever." She sighed. "Long ago, I was deeply in love, but the man I loved changed." She turned her brown eyes to me. "Love is fleeting and your chance to be happy with your mate might not be there forever."

"It isn't that simple," I whispered.

"Simple is a choice," she said. "If I were you, I would tell him how you feel, I would tell him about the mating bond, and I would do everything in my power to love him for as long as I could."

KEERAN

WHEN I ARRIVED AT BAGATHA'S OLD COTTAGE, I EXPECTED TO find vampires and the witchguard keeping watch, but the forest and the clearing around the little house was eerily quiet.

"Good evening," I said as I entered the cottage and found Thea and Drake seated on the couch, as if they were the homeowners, brewing tea and waiting for guests.

A cold chill ran down my spine when Thea looked at me, sans smile. "We need to talk," she said, her voice hard.

I sat down on an armchair across the coffee table, bracing myself. "What is it?"

"We heard some interesting news involving a warlock named Soren," Drake said, his tone and gaze as hard as Thea's.

"Then we also heard Isalia, who is now the alpha of the Dark Vale pack, is in the mix," Thea said. "Care to explain what's going on?"

"And where's Luana?" Drake asked. "Last I heard, she was

with you after losing her title. I sent a message to her too, but nobody can find her."

Shit. I let out a long sigh and told them all that had occurred since I had left the Silverblood Estate. I told them about bumping into Luana after Isalia invaded her pack and challenged her—how she won by cheating. I told them about stopping by the Wildthorn coven, then the Bonecrown coven, where I learned about my mother and my father and the prophecy—though I omitted my latest discovery of going evil when I killed my father. I even told them about saving Farrah from the Bonecrown witches and having her help us. I also told them about the lies Soren had told me and his real plan: to kill the witches, including Thea and Aurora, and seize power for himself. I told them Soren was still looking for my mother and that he wanted me to join him in his quest. How I said no, which led to our duel and how he fled after. Then, I told them Luana and Wyatt had left Dark Witch Manor to return to their pack, promising to contact me when they needed my help.

"That was a week ago and I haven't heard from them since," I said. "I was just out in the woods around the manor this morning, looking for clues."

"Did you find anything?" Drake asked.

I nodded. "Blood and signs of struggle. I think someone attacked Luana and Wyatt."

Drake and Thea exchange a meaningful glance. "Soren?" Thea asked.

"Maybe Isalia," Drake said. He turned his icy green gaze to me. "Anything else we should know?"

I shook my head. "That's all. I swear." Facing them like this, I felt like I was in court, being judged for a crime.

"How many do you need?" Drake asked.

I was confused. "What do you mean?"

"How many vampires and witches," Drake clarified. "If you can't solve the situation by yourself, we'll send our people to help. How many do you need?"

A mix of frustration and rage snaked into my core. "I can handle it myself." Could I? My warlocks didn't seem inclined to help me. Maybe if I had a few vampires and witches on my side, things would go more smoothly. But would that help my position as warlock lord? I feared that if my warlocks saw me working with other supernaturals instead of them, they would trust me less and less. "I will handle this myself."

Once more, Thea and Drake exchanged a look. I remembered Bagatha once told them that because of the Immortal Vow, they would one day be able to communicate inside their minds. Had they reached that point already?

"We'll give you a few days," Thea said.

Drake nodded. "If you can't solve this by then, we'll send you a few of our soldiers."

I inhaled deeply, not just frustrated with the situation and a little mad at them, but also disappointed in myself.

"Keeran," Thea started, her voice normal again, almost too sweet. "We're glad you found other warlocks and became the warlock lord, but you have to understand, we're trying to create a peaceful world. Suddenly, it's all getting out of hand again."

"Our biggest concern is Aurora," Drake continued for her. "We want to create a peaceful world where she can be a safe. That comes before her duties as the queen of all witches."

"I understand," I muttered, feeling like I was a little kid being reprimanded by the teacher at school. Even I, growing up as a servant in a witch coven, had frequented the little school that was set up in their servants' quarters. Now, all that was gone, of course, since Thea had freed all the servants.

Beside these two powerful supernaturals, I felt like a failure.

Thea and Drake stood.

"We'll be waiting for news." Thea walked to me and I stood, half expecting she would slap me in the face and confess how disappointed she was on me. Instead, she hugged me tight. "I'm glad you're okay. Please don't hesitate to call us."

I relaxed a little. "Thank you."

She placed a soft kiss on my cheek, then walked out of the cottage.

Drake nodded at me and marched after her. But at the door, he paused and looked back at me. "I can see you're hurting."

"Excuse me?" I asked, confused. What was he talking about? My mother? My father? The prophecy?

"About Luana," he said, his voice low. "I can see you like her. Well, love her."

I swallowed. Was it that easy to see? "Yes, it's hurting to not know where she is and what's going on."

"I'm sure you'll find her," Drake said. "But do me a favor. Once you find her, tell her how you feel."

I frowned. Why was he saying that?

Drake zipped out of the cottage with his super speed, and I was left alone.

After taking a deep breath and composing myself, I started back to Dark Witch Manor. I made a mental note of all I had to do: get a team together, find Luana and Wyatt, reinforce the manor's defenses, and prepare for a fight with Soren.

My gut twisted. Even Thea and Drake wanted me to deal with Soren, to kill him. If I didn't, they would.

Was there really no way to escape this cursed prophecy? I had to find a way, because now what scared me the most wasn't just killing my father, but also becoming evil like him.

I stepped on a thin branch, and its loud snapping sound echoing through the forest sent my heart into a race. I had been so distracted that a freaking simple sound like that had scared me.

I slowed down, breathing deeply.

So messed up. I was so messed up.

Enough of this nonsense. Time was of the essence, and I had to get back to the manor fast.

I sped up as the air around me changed, as if a thick veil had fallen over it.

I frowned.

A growl came from my side a second before a wolf jumped out from behind a bush and landed on top of me.

# 9

---

LUANA

My days in Unity passed by in a blur. I had been out of the bed for three days now, and I had never felt better. If I shut out all the bad things going on beyond the village, I could spend my days smiling and having a good time.

In the mornings, I had breakfast with Almae, then went out for a stroll around the village. I walked by the stands in the market, and got to know the merchants and their family. I knew most of their names and what they did for the community. I had even been invited to dinner by one of the werewolf families who had moved here a few years ago and couldn't be happier about not having an alpha and pack rules to follow.

In the afternoons, I napped—a luxury I never had before—then went for a swim at the waterfall. At night, I met up with Almae for dinner again. After dinner, we had tea, talked some more, and I went to bed early.

It was the perfect life.

I couldn't help but plot it all. I would build a house for myself, come up with some business I could contribute to the village, and create my own stand at the market. Who knew?

Maybe someday I would even fall in love with another lone wolf and have beautiful puppies.

At those thoughts, the mating bond tugged at my heart, telling me I was lying to myself. All I had ever done was ruin everything. Here, I wouldn't be a burden to anyone. Here, I could hide forever, and if I ended up alone until I died, so be it.

It was a nice price to pay.

As I swam under the waterfall, I let the water wash away my worries. I was happy here, calm, relaxed. That was all that mattered.

When I dragged myself out of the water and sat down on a big rock on the lake's bank, I felt energized. I lifted my chin up and soaked in the warm sun as it dried off my skin.

"You seem much better," Almae said as she took a seat on the rock beside me.

I looked at her, a soft smile at my lips. "I am. I think I'm recovered now." I grabbed the towel from the side and wrapped it around myself. Although I was wearing a bikini she had found for me, and I wasn't timid about my body, I didn't think she liked seeing so much of my skin. "I've never felt better."

She nodded. "I can see that." A line marred her forehead. "Are you planning on staying?"

The way she said it … "Why? Am I not allow to?"

"No, that's not it," she said. "Of course, you are. You're welcome to stay."

My body tensed. So long calm and relaxation. "But?"

She let out a long sigh. "Nobody can hide from their fate, no matter how far you run. But … if you want to stay, you're welcome here."

"What is my fate?" My tone turned bitter, despite my best

efforts to stay neutral. "To become an alpha of a pack of wolves that is almost gone?" Isalia had killed over fifty percent of our pack, and the rest still alive had gone mad along with her, which made me think: Did I still want to be their alpha? Could I still save them? "Or to be a consort for the warlock lord?" Which was ridiculous. I had been sure that if I was alpha my wolves would never agree to a warlock being my mate, and I doubted Keeran's warlocks would like having a werewolf in their midst.

"The right path usually isn't the easiest," Almae said. I groaned. Really? Life lessons right now? She shrugged. "To me, it doesn't make a difference what you choose. Just know that I'll support you, no matter what."

At least those words warmed my insides a little. In the past few days, Almae had become a constant in my life. A pillar of support and understanding. I could talk about anything with her. She was a mix of a good friend and a mother, and I really treasured that.

"Thanks," I muttered. My soul and heart weren't splitting in two. They were tearing in three, four, maybe five pieces.

"Oh," Almae said. She put a hand over her chest.

"What happened?" I asked, turning to her.

"A—" Her hand dropped and her head lolled back. Her arms and shoulders trembled. Moon be damned, was she having convulsions?

"Almae?"

I hopped off the rock and grabbed her face. I gasped and almost dropped her. Her eyes were white. No irises, no pupils. All white. And her lips moved fast as if she was saying something, but no sound came out. Moon help me, what should I do?

"Help!" I yelled, hoping there was someone nearby who

would hear me. Maybe the other people in Unity had seen this before and knew what to do, because other than hold her so she didn't hurt herself, I didn't know what to do. "Hel—"

Almae's hand shot forward and grabbed my wrist. I almost jumped back from the scare.

"It's okay," she muttered, her voice weak. She blinked and her eyes came back to normal. Her body stopped shaking. "I'm fine now." She let go of my wrist and pressed a hand over her stomach.

I took a step back to take a better look at her. She said she was fine, but she was pale, and she looked like she had aged at least twenty years. "What was that? What happened?"

She took a long breath. "I had a vision."

I frowned. "A vision?"

"Yes, a vision." She reached for me. "I always feel sick after having visions. Would you mind helping me to my bed?"

I took hold of her hand and wrapped her arm around my shoulders. With my werewolf strength, I was able to carry most of her weight, even if Almae insisted on walking. Slowly, we made our way up the path. The few supernaturals who walked by us stopped and asked if Almae was okay. They didn't seem worried, which led me to believe they had seen this before. At least, that told me I shouldn't be too worried either.

Or should I?

Almae remained quiet as we made our way to her house. I helped her to her room, and as she climbed into bed, I grabbed a glass of cold water for her.

"Here." I left the glass on the nightstand beside her bed. "You should drink it."

"Later." She shook her head. "I need to tell you something first."

I hoped she was going to tell me about this vision, because I was curious. However, to be honest, I preferred she didn't exert herself. "It's okay. Just rest first."

She shook her head. "I'm okay, really. This is just an after-effect of my visions. I'm used to it. Give me a couple of hours, and I'll be fine."

"Then you can tell me whatever it is in a couple of hours."

"Luana," she said, her voice harsher than I had ever heard it. "Listen to me." I stilled. "It was more than a vision. It was a prophecy. It showed me that Unity is in danger of being destroyed by a she-wolf and her female pack." I gasped. It was Isalia and the remainder of the Dark Vale pack. "And that alongside this alpha, a dark warlock will rise to destroy the Silverblood coven and all the other witches, unless another warlock stops him."

My stomach twisted and I felt like I would be sick. "Moon be cursed."

"If you're wondering if this prophecy is about Isalia and Soren and Keeran, let me tell you, it is."

This didn't make sense. "But ... prophecies? You're some kind of oracle?"

She nodded. "Let's say that seeing prophecies is my main witch power." She sighed and continued, "I was the one who made the first prophecy about Keeran long ago. Like that one is on its way of becoming true, this one will too."

My spine straightened. "No, we can't let that happen. Has any of your prophecies been wrong?"

"It's kind of hard to tell. I once had a prophecy that was changed."

"What do you mean?"

She glanced out the window. "I once had a prophecy of a young witch who would be kidnapped, and her powers would be stolen. Because I was afraid for her, I told her that. She prepared herself. She trained. When the time came, she killed her kidnapper before he could take her. But ... before it happened, I saw the changes in another prophecy."

"So, your first prophecy was rescinded, and the second one prevailed."

Returning her eyes to me, she nodded. "Proving that my prophecies always come true."

"And right now, you're saying Isalia and Soren will come and destroy Unity."

"Unless someone kills them first and changes the prophecy," she said, her eyes locked on mine.

The meaning of her words sank in, and I took a step back. "You want me to kill Isalia."

"Not only you," she said. "Don't try it alone. Go back to Keeran and your friends. Gather them and change this horrible fate."

In the end, I had no choice. As much as I wanted to stay, I couldn't. I had to go and face my enemies. If it wasn't for Keeran and me, then it would be for this beautiful place and its safety.

I let out a long breath. "I can't believe I really have to go."

"You don't have to," Almae said, her tone soft. "I'm suggesting you go, not ordering you to go. You can tell me you don't want to, and I won't force you."

"But someone will have to go."

She nodded. "I will send someone, yes. I won't let them get close to Unity, even if I'm the one who goes after them."

Who would she send? I had been here a handful of days and had seen only a few men who acted like guards, walking around in crappy uniform and crappier weapons. To be honest, they didn't look like they had been trained as real warriors. I bet they knew how to cast a few spells and use their abilities well, but not enough to defend Unity if necessary.

And this was all on me. If Isalia came this way, it was because she had found me here. I had to leave and stop her before she got close.

I raised my chin, gathering the courage I thought I had abandoned. "I'll go."

## 10

---



THE ENRAGED WOLF SNAPPED ITS SHARP TEETH RIGHT IN FRONT of my face. Channeling my power, I blasted the wolf's chest. He yelped as he was pushed back by the force of the impact, and I pushed to my feet.

I conjured another bolt to attack him, but the red glow in my hand illuminated the wolf and I gasped, dropping my magic.

"Wyatt?"

Could it be? Where was Luana, then? And why was he attacking me?

The wolf jumped at me again. I sidestepped him and conjured a small ball of light in my hand. I didn't have his enhanced vision and I didn't want to hurt him. "Wyatt, it's me. Keeran." Why didn't he recognize me?

I bounced the light ball up, and it hovered a couple of feet from my head, illuminating more of the area. And then I saw it. Wyatt's eyes. They were savage. As if he were a real wolf, not a werewolf. Like he was driven by bloodlust, nothing more. It was as though he was a monster and wouldn't stop until I was dead. Foam gathered at the corners of his mouth, and he snarled at me again.

I channeled my power, ready to cast a shield to protect me from his attacks, and a new power brushed against mine. A thin but firm magic. I searched for it and gasped when I found it in Wyatt. He had been bewitched.

"What did they do to you?" I whispered as I saw the injuries matting his brown fur. My gut tightened. Wyatt lunged at me again. I cast a shield. He slammed against the shield and fell back on his side. A yelp ripped through his throat. "Sorry!" I called, hating to hurt him more.

Shit, I had to break this spell somehow.

As Wyatt recovered and turned to jump at me again, I called my magic and pushed it on him. Like a heavy blanket, I forced it down over Wyatt, keeping him contained on the ground. He raged, snarling and snapping his sharp teeth at me.

While holding on to that spell, I closed my eyes and focused. Like I had done with Farrah before, I searched for the enchantment taking hold of him, so I could break it. But when I found it, my shoulders deflated. Although it had appeared to be a weak spell at first, it wasn't. It was thick and firm and etched deep in him. I tugged at it, reciting every enchantment I could remember trying to break it, but nothing worked.

Breaking free of my spell, Wyatt shot up and snarled at me.

Shit.

He lunged at me and I twisted to the side, his teeth grazing the air an inch from my shoulder.

"Wyatt, stop," I begged, as if I could break the enchantment with begging. "I don't want to hurt you."

He didn't stop. To defend myself, I cast shield after shield, but that only made him madder as he was pushed back. He didn't give up and kept coming, slamming his body against the shields.

The only solution I saw was to cast a bolt that would stun him, but not kill him. It would hurt like hell, but it was better than the alternative.

Channeling my magic, I conjured a small red bolt in my hand.

Wyatt advanced on me.

A second wolf arched over the bushes and barreled into Wyatt, pushing him back several feet.

I gasped as the second wolf halted in front of me, facing Wyatt.

It was Luana and she was defending me.

"It's Wyatt," I told her. "But he has been enchanted."

Wyatt turned to Luana, his fangs bared. Luana stomped her paw on the ground and let out a low growl. Wyatt advanced a step. Luana's growl increased. Wyatt stopped. Her growl grew louder. Wyatt lowered his head.

Then Luana took a step forward and let out a long howl.

Wyatt spun around and took off, disappearing among the trees. Luana took off after him.

"No, Luana, wait!" I called, but she was gone.

With the light ball hovering over my head, I chased after her, but in her wolf form, she was much faster than me.

For a moment, I panicked. I had just found the two of them, and in a matter of minutes, I had lost them again.

What if it took me a week to find them again? What if I didn't find them again?

Just as I thought I would break down in despair, bushes to

my left ruffled and Luana stepped out of the shadows, still in her wolf form.

I stopped breathing, but when Luana shifted back into her human body, I let out a long, relieved breath. My eyes filled with tears. Holy shit, I had been so freaking worried.

I took off my cloak, and with my eyes locked on hers, placed it around her shoulders.

"Thanks," she whispered, tightening the fabric around herself.

I couldn't help it. I reached for her, cupping her face. "You have no idea how I've felt these past few days. I thought something really bad had happened to you."

She tilted her head, pressing her cheek to my hand. "I'm here now."

I didn't care if we had parted on not so great terms. All that mattered now was that she was here and that was all I needed.

Wrapping my arm around her waist, I pulled her to me and crushed my mouth to hers. I thought she would resist me, but Luana melted in my arms instantly. She parted her lips for me, and I devoured her.

I had missed her, but I only realized it had physically hurt when she was like this—safe in my arms. Her mouth tasted like sin, and the thin cloak around her body didn't help with my increasing desire.

If I didn't have so many questions, I wouldn't have stopped. But as it was, Luana was the one to break the kiss. Apprehension clutched at my chest. I was sure she would step back and pretend nothing happen. Instead, she took a small step back and looked up at me, a smile tugging at her lips.

An urge to kiss her again hit me hard and fast, but I pushed it back.

Focusing on our current situation, I looked around. "Where's Wyatt?"

"He ran from me," she said, her brows curled down. "I wanted to make him submit, so you could try to break whatever spell is on him, but he fled."

"I tried breaking the spell already," I confessed. "I couldn't do it." Tears brimmed her eyes. I reached for her again. "What is it?"

"I thought he was dead," she whispered.

A knot formed between my brows. I had no idea what they had been through these past few days, but so far, I could only imagine it was a lot. "What happened?"

She shook her head. "I don't want to talk about that now. Can we just go back to Dark Witch Manor first?"

"Of course." I offered her my arm. "Shall we?"

Wiping at her eyes, Luana offered me a half-grin. Then, she slapped my arm away. "We shall."

She marched on and I rushed to catch up with her.

***

THE WARLOCKS WEREN'T HAPPY TO SEE LUANA. DESPITE HAVING looked for her and Wyatt with me, they had done it because I had ordered them to, not because they cared about them.

I asked Flavius to get some food ready and take it to my bedroom, before I escorted Luana that way.

After she and Wyatt left, Zell had shown me to my father's suite, but for some reason, I didn't feel comfortable taking it. Instead, I stayed in the suite I had been given when we first had arrived at Dark Witch Manor. It wasn't as large or fancy as the warlock lord's chambers, but I didn't care. This simpler suite—with a four-poster queen bed, nightstands, a loveseat, and a small end table—was more my style. And I still had a full closet and a big bathroom. What more did I need?

Without thinking, I guided Luana inside my suite.

"You can take a shower there." I pointed to the bathroom's door. "I'll grab some clothes for you."

"Thanks," she muttered, dragging her feet into the bathroom.

She shut the door, and I let out a long breath.

I went to the suite across the hallway, where she had stayed before she left, and picked out a handful of things from the closet—pants, shirt, a set that looked like comfortable pajamas, and even a casual dress. Who knew what she was in the mood for? Although, I thought I had only seen Luana in a dress once at Thea's and Drake's wedding, and even then, it had been a modern dress, instead of those princess gowns.

I spread the clothes out on my bed and sat down on the mattress, waiting. Each time I remembered that she was showering in my bathroom, my heartbeat sped up. I had seen her naked many times. Why did knowing she was naked just behind the door make me so nervous?

I hoped the sound of the water was enough to muffle the freaking beat of my heart, otherwise Luana would know how anxious and lustful I was right now.

A moment later, the bathroom's door opened and Luana stepped out, wrapped in a white towel, her wet hair curled around her shoulders.

I swallowed hard.

"Hm, the clothes?"

"Here." I gestured toward my bed and stepped back. Did I

expect her to get dressed in front of me? Of course not. Stupid me, I should have given her the clothes before she disappeared into the bathroom. "I'm going to, uh, wait outside."

I spun around, toward the door.

"Keeran."

I froze. Slowly, I glanced at her from over my shoulder. "Yes?"

"Thank you," she whispered.

My brows furrowed. "For?"

"For searching for Wyatt and me." She shrugged. "For not giving up on me. Just ... for being you."

Her words clutched at my chest and squeezed tight. It felt like a pull, tugging me straight toward her.

I couldn't stop myself.

With my eyes on hers, I stalked to her, my steps slow, my gaze unwavering. She didn't balk; she didn't retreat. She remained in her spot, until I was inches from her.

Heat surged through me as she tilted her chin up, angling her head toward mine, but she didn't go any farther. I knew what she was doing. She was letting me know she wanted this, but she was waiting for me to take the next step.

I closed my eyes for a moment, filling my mind with her. With her face, smile, her scent, and her touch. Nothing else mattered, no one from the past could get to me. There was only Luana and I adored her.

Luana took a step back as I opened my eyes. Her face fell, as if she had been defeated.

"Where do you think you're going?" I stepped into her, this time pressing my body to hers, and wound my arms around her waist. She let out a low gasp. "Unless you—"

She rose on her tiptoes and pressed her lips to mine.

That was all I needed to know.

I closed my mouth around hers and kissed her with all I had—all the love, all the lust, all the respect. There was a time when I thought I would never be able to feel this way for anyone, but Luana had come into my world, sneaked in slowly, left strong roots, and now she practically owned my soul.

Devouring her mouth, I pushed against her, and she took a couple steps back, until her back was pressed against the wall.

I had no intention of breaking the kiss, but then her towel fell.

I couldn't resist. I pulled away, just enough to look at her. Really look at her. I had seen her naked hundreds of times before. I knew her body was beautiful and her skin smooth, but back then, I was trying to be polite. I halted any other kind of thoughts.

Now was different. Now, I could look at her and let my desire, my lust rise. I could lick my lips as I stared at her full breasts, her thin waist, the hard muscles in her stomach, her long, lean legs.

All of my blood rushed to my pelvis.

"You're so freaking gorgeous," I whispered before dipping into her and closing my mouth around one of her breasts.

Gasping, Luana arched her back. She clutched at me, her nails sinking into my shoulders, as I licked the curves of her breast, and sucked on her nipple. She tasted so freaking good.

Needing more of her, I slid my hands down to her hips.

This wasn't enough. I spun her around and pressed her against the wall, her back to me. She gasped again as I pushed my hips into her ass.

I lowered my head to her neck and inhaled deeply. Her scent teased my senses and only made me crazier. I snaked my arms around her and closed my hands over her breasts. I pinched her nipples, ripping a yelp from her, before moving my hands down.

Luana tensed against me for a second while I found her center and slipped my finger inside her. Then, I slipped another finger and started pumping into her, and she melted into me. I bit her neck while I explored her with my fingers.

Using my thumb, I played with her clit. I was about to carry her to the bed and finish this with my mouth, when I felt her walls clenching against my fingers, her body tensing against mine.

She was close. Without mercy, I teased her clit and thrusted my fingers into her, as hard and fast as I could.

Luana cried out as she came, her body trembling, trapped between the wall and me.

So freaking hot.

I picked her up in my arms and carried her to the bed. I deposited her in the center and stepped back. Under her half-closed gaze, I took off my clothes and crawled over her.

I brushed my lips on her stomach, on her breasts, on her neck—

She flipped us over and straddled me.

"My turn to enjoy the view," she said, pressing her wet center on my hard-on. Holy hell, the sensation. I gritted my teeth while she grazed her nails over the muscles of my chest and stomach, her eyes glinting with desire. "So hot."

I couldn't take much more of this.

I reached for her, intent on grasping her waist and slipping inside her, but Luana was faster. She splayed her hands on my chest and slowly sat on me, taking me in deep.

I sucked in a sharp breath as her hot, wet core pressed

against me. Holy shit, this was ... I had no words. I didn't want to move ever again. I didn't want her to leave ever again.

And yet, I needed her to move.

As if reading my mind, Luana lifted her ass a little, ever so slowly, then slammed down back on me.

A string of curses bloomed on the tip of my tongue.

"Are you okay?" she asked, her voice breathy, as she lifted her ass once more.

"Okay? I'm wonderful." This time I did reach for her and grasped her waist. "Just ... don't stop."

A sly smile took over her lips. And she moved. For the love of—

She moved up and down, taking me deeper and harder with each thrust. So freaking good. I had had sex hundreds of times before, but I had never ever felt like this. All those times, I had been forced to sleep with the witches. I felt nothing for them.

Now, with Luana, everything was different. She didn't need to force me. I wanted this probably more than she did. And I felt something for her. Something real, something strong. And the more time she spent riding me, the stronger and more real it felt.

My chest felt full, too full, as if it could explode with desire and love, and everything in between, at any second. Was this how sex felt with someone you liked? When you wanted it? I knew it was supposed to be so good; it felt like out of this world, but this ... it was more.

I pressed a hand to my chest as this new feeling, this crazy feeling, threatened to choke me.

Needing to take charge, I pushed up, hooked an arm around Luana's waist, and spin us around. I laid her down on the bed and pressed my body against hers. She smiled at me as I pressed my hips into hers.

She was so freaking perfect.

I lowered my lips to hers and kissed her while I thrust inside her. She let me consume her mouth as I rode her, taking as much as I could of her. Her nails scratched my back, sending shivers down my spine and curling my toes.

I couldn't take much more of this. I deepened the kiss as I pushed against her, harder and deeper with each stroke. I felt myself breaking apart as the ecstasy took over me.

Luana cried out, and her body broke into tremors under me. I felt her walls clench around me and it was all I needed. I gritted my teeth and buried my face in her neck as I came.

Luana ran her hands on my back as my body relaxed. "Are you okay?"

I lifted my head and looked into her worried eyes. I smiled at her. "Never been better."

She smiled back at me, and that smile only confirmed one thing: I was crazy about her. Had been for a while now. I would do anything in my power to protect her, to love her, to make her happy.

Even if that meant killing our enemies myself.

## 11

SLEEPING IN KEERAN'S ARMS WAS EVEN BETTER THAN MY NIGHTS in Unity. Even though I was unsure of his feelings for me, I didn't think I had ever felt safer or more complete.

Giving in to the mating bond and making love to my mate had been incredible. It was a shame Keeran still didn't know what he was to me. And for now, I had no plans of telling him.

Keeran stirred, rubbing his nose and short beard on my neck. A shiver ran down my body and settled between my thighs. By the moon, if he continued like that, I would end up attacking him before he was fully awake.

"Good morning," he mumbled, his mouth brushing against my skin.

I twisted away from him. "Morning."

Keeran wound his arm around me and pulled closer. "Are you trying to run from me again?"

I chuckled. "I wouldn't dare."

He propped his elbow up and rested his head on his hand. "Did you sleep well?"

I nestled closer, loving the feel of his warm body against mine. "Very. How about you?"

He let out a long breath. "I don't think I have slept that well in over a month."

A proud smile tugged at my lips. "So now you know what to do. Call me up before bed every night. We can fool around and then you'll sleep like an angel."

He looked appalled. "You think that was fooling around?"

I shrugged, loving to tease him. Better than anyone, I knew we hadn't been fooling around, but I wasn't ready to talk about that yet. "Call it whatever you want."

"I'm just glad you're here," he whispered. His eyes skimmed my face, then he traced a finger over the scar on my cheek and neck. I turned away. "Don't hide. I happen to like your scar." He placed a soft kiss on my cheek, right above where the thin white line started. "You're still beautiful." He pulled back, his eyes on mine. "You'll always be."

I couldn't take it. The emotion in his gaze, the sweet tone of his voice, the way his body was pressed against mine, I couldn't take it. I scooted back, and holding on to the sheets, sat up in bed, my back pressed to the headboard. "We need to talk."

A frown formed between his brows. Slowly, Keeran sat up on the bed beside me. "Are you going to tell me what happened while you were gone?"

Nodding, I inhaled deeply. "Wyatt and I had just left Dark Witch Manor when we were attacked. We didn't see them coming, and we didn't know who it was until we woke up in cells hours later." I kept going with my tale, telling him everything. Soren and his plan to lure Keeran there by using me. The torture sessions. Isalia's invasion and their weird alliance. The moment she was going to kill me. The smoke that filled the room. The person who saved me. Waking through Unity and finding out Wyatt had been killed during the rescue—though I had found out that wasn't true. Meeting Almae and discovering Unity. "That place ... it's perfect. All kinds of supernaturals live there as if they were humans, even a few warlocks. No one tries to take advantage of the others. There are no evil leaders, or bloody battles, or diabolic plans. I thought such a place would be a faraway dream, but it's much closer than I could ever imagine."

"That sounds more like a dream than a real place."

"I know. I felt the same way when I first woke up there, but it's real," I said, having problems in disguising my excitement from my words. "And Almae, the leader ... she has the gift of prophecies."

Keeran's eyes went wide. "Prophecies. It would be good to have a witch by our side with that gift."

I shook my head. "Almae doesn't want to join us. She wants to stay there and keep Unity hidden. Actually, while I was there, she foresaw that Unity would be attacked by a pack of she-wolves."

"Isalia," he muttered.

"Yes. Isalia would go there, trying to find me," I told him. "So, I left. I want to face Isalia and take her down before she finds Unity."

"I understand, but I can't help but be disappointed. I wish she and the supernaturals at Unity would join us. Especially the warlocks. Having more numbers would increase our odds of winning."

I reached over and placed my hand on his warm skin, right above his heart. "We can do this. You and me and our friends. We can take Isalia and Soren down ourselves." I paused as sadness washed over me. "We also need to save

Wyatt." It wasn't only being brainwashed that I was worried about. As far as I knew, there were hunters whose sole purpose was to kill all kinds of supernaturals, even when they weren't evil. If Wyatt ran into one of them, he might end up in even more trouble.

His eyes stared into mine with so much fervor. "We'll save him." He pressed his hand over mine, and I could feel the steady beat of his heart against my palm. "Let's do it." He stretched and placed a quick kiss on my lips before jumping from the bed. "Let's get ready. I'll call a meeting so we can organize everything."

I stayed in bed a few more minutes, watching as Keeran strolled to one side of the bedroom, then another, gathering his things and getting dressed—black pants and matching shirt and his cloak—seemingly driven with purpose.

My breath caught.

He was so handsome and he looked so imposing with those clothes covering his tall, wide frame. His five o'clock shadow had to be enchanted so it was always the same length, and so was his hair since it barely moved no matter where we were and what we were doing. It all just added to the perfect and whole feeling pressuring my chest.

I should tell him. Right now. I should tell him about my feelings and about the mating bond. This was my opportunity, because who knew what would happen next? Depending on his coven's answer, we would be marching to battle by the end of the day, and I wouldn't have another opportunity until everything was said and done.

I opened my mouth, but no words came out. I couldn't do it. If I told him, it would ruin everything.

Reluctantly, I dragged my ass from the bed and started getting ready.

AN HOUR LATER, KEERAN AND I WAITED IN THE THRONE ROOM. Slowly, the warlocks filled the place and waited for whatever had brought them here.

Meanwhile, I felt their gazes on me. Some looked at me with sympathy, and others openly glared at me. I knew what they were thinking—that I was a thorn in Keeran's side.

Focusing on the short temper in my wolf blood, I stood my ground and didn't cower at them.

Once every warlock was present, Zell stepped forward. "Have you called us, my lord?"

"Yes." Keeran puffed his chest, looking proud and strong. But I was the only one here who could hear the rapid beat of his heart. He was nervous addressing the warlocks, of telling them what to do. "I've learned that Soren joined forces with Isalia, the powerful and mad alpha of the Dark Vale pack." Mutters filled the room. "Together, they form an impressive faction. With a former warlock lord and an alpha wolf, we all know they will come for us. Because of that, I believe we should attack them first."

"We have no problems with the werewolves," someone said from the crowd.

My blood curdled, but I kept myself quiet—I was proud at being able to control my temper.

"I think that has changed since Isalia joined Soren and his warlocks," Keeran said. There was a hard edge to his voice, and I knew he too was reigning in his temper. "They are together now, and they will attack us together."

"This isn't fair," another warlock said. With my hearing, I knew exactly where the voice was coming from, but I tried not looking at him. If I did, my rage might spike, and I wouldn't be able to control myself. "We're dozens of warlocks and there's only one wolf here."

"And she's a guest," someone else said.

"Or maybe she's a spy," another one said.

The rage in my veins spiked and I took a step forward. Keeran put his arm out, like a barrier I couldn't cross. At that moment, I wanted to rip his arm off, then tear through the throats of these insolent warlocks.

"What I me—"

"You're missing the point here," I said, cutting Keeran off. "What you have to understand is that we are in this together now. Isalia and Soren are one pack, one coven. They don't care about who's a warlock and who's a werewolf. If you're not on their side, you're an enemy, thus you need to be killed." Gasps echoed around me. What? They thought I would stay quiet? "The only way for us to defeat them is if we work together too."

"You and what army?" a warlock asked. I recognized his voice, as he had made another nasty comment before, but I didn't know his name.

That sucked. "Once I defeat Isalia and become the alpha again, I can command the other wolves to stand down." Just like we had done in the battle at DuMoir Castle.

Zell turned to the other warlocks. "I think Lord Keeran and Luana are right." The room went silent. "The more time we give to our enemies, the stronger they will be. We need to attack them now."

Beside me, Keeran frowned and his heart picked up again. Clearing his throat, he said, "We're going to attack the Chateau of the Cursed tonight." The murmurs began again. "I have one condition, though."

I stared at Keeran. A condition? What was he talking about?

"Which is?" Zell asked.

"We won't kill Soren," Keeran said, loud and clear. "We'll imprison him instead."

Zell's brows furrowed, and he let out a long breath. "I was afraid it would come to that."

Keeran shook his head once. "What do you mean?"

Zell lifted his hand high and a black light shot from it. Several warlocks stepped forward from the crowd, black bolts in their hands. I gasped as I realized they were the same ones who had saved me from Virion, Soren's right hand, before.

My surprise was replaced by fury, and my wolf woke up inside me, begging to shift and attack.

A black bolt appeared in Zell's open palm and he pointed it at Keeran. "This is me taking control."

It took me a moment to react.

I stepped back, my hands up and ready for a spell. "What the ...?" I stared at Zell. "What's going on?"

Zell shook his head. "I've had enough of your hesitant behavior. If you're not going to take down Soren, then we'll finish it."

"I am going to take down Soren, just not the way you want me to," I said through gritted teeth.

"I was willing to follow you," Zell said, sounding disappointed. "I saw your power and know your legacy; I knew about the prophecy. I believed in you. I thought you would be great. But you won't, unless you're able to put your morals aside and do what's necessary."

"By the moon," Luana snarled.

I grabbed her arm and held her back before she attacked him. "I've killed enough. I will not kill any more unless it's to defend my coven, my friends, and myself."

"Don't you see?" Zell tapped his temple with his index

finger. "Killing Soren is defending the entire world. He needs to be stopped, and not by imprisoning him. By killing him."

"Death isn't always the answer!" I shouted. Why did our world have to be so bloody and deadly? Why did everything have to end in battles and betrayals and death?

"You're a coward," Zell spat.

"How dare you?" Luana advanced, and again I had to hold her arms to keep her back. She had partially shifted, with her wolf eyes and fangs showing. If they didn't stop, I didn't know what would happen.

Zell beckoned to Luana. "Aside from that, everyone here can see you're putting a werewolf before the needs of your own coven."

Luana growled.

"This is bullshit." I felt my power waking up, even though I hadn't consciously called for it. My magic responded to my anger.

"Stand down," Zell said, his voice rising. "Stand down and let me take over. I'll become the new warlock lord and I'll take this coven where it needs to go."

I stared at Zell. So that was his cursed plan all along. He played with me, but his intention was to become warlock lord instead of me. That was why he said he didn't mind if I killed Soren and became evil, because he would take care of me before I turned against him. And now Zell was making me look like a freaking idiot in front of the coven, so they would willingly choose him instead of me.

And to think I had considered abdicating my title for a more capable warlock. So much for any consideration, when the people you trusted stabbed you in the back.

I took in a deep breath and braced myself. "I won't stand down."

Black magic enveloped Zell's hands. "Then I challenge you to a duel for the title of warlock lord."

He didn't give me a second to think, much less to answer. Throwing his hands out, Zell sent the magic toward me.

I cast a shield in front of Luana and myself, but Zell's blasts were fast and hard, and the shield broke a few seconds later.

I channeled more of my magic. "Stop this, Zell."

"I'll only stop when you surrender," the warlock said. Black shadows swirled around him. "I'll give you one more chance: surrender and walk away."

Did he really think I would turn my back and leave now? Until a few weeks ago, I believed I was the only warlock alive. I had found men like me, a group where I could belong, and he was asking me to leave. The thought of stepping aside had crossed my mind, but I hadn't considered running away. My idea had been to give the title to some other warlock, but remain here.

I wouldn't run away.

Gritting my teeth, I pulled back my arms and threw red bolts at him. Zell easily waved them away. Black darts flew out of his hands in an arc, directed at my chest. I jumped out of the way.

A few yards from me, Luana let out a low growl and shifted.

"No!" I yelled. She stared at me with round eyes. "This is my fight."

She clenched her fists, but took a few steps back. It was easy to see she didn't like it, but she wouldn't interfere.

Meanwhile, Zell sent more of his magic toward me. I moved out of the way of several blasts, and brought up another shield to catch my breath and summon more magic.

Laughter echoed through the throne room. Zell's chest shook as if I had told a joke. "Keeran, I've trained you," he said, his voice high. "I know all of your moves and tricks. For instance, I know you always put up a shield when you need time to think or to channel your magic." Zell extended his hand and a small ball of black magic appeared in his palm. "And I also know that if I cast enough power, I can break the shield and hit you." He threw the black bolt.

The shield broke, and I had to twist out of the way to avoid being hit. But Zell was ready. He sent one bolt after another, and I danced and twisted, my steps pushing me back. A couple of bolts grazed my shoulders and I gritted my teeth, forcing myself to endure the pain.

"You should surrender, Keeran," Galroth said, his voice low. He stood tall beside Zell, but his brown eyes were downcast, as if he was afraid of looking directly at me. "We don't want to hurt you."

"No." Zell shook his head. "I gave him a chance to surrender. That chance is gone."

The warlock opened his arms wide and magic thrummed through the room. With the amount of magic he was summoning, his next strike would certainly kill me, even if it only grazed my shoulder again.

Perhaps I could raise a shield and lessen the impact of—

Luana growled and shifted again.

Without hesitation, Galroth turned to her and threw a black bolt at her.

Luana yelped as the bolt hit her squared in the chest, pushing her back a few steps and stopping her shifting. She fell on her knees, panting.

Rage consumed me.

I sent a red bolt at Galroth. Zell pushed him out of the

way, but not before the bolt grazed past both of their arms, leaving a trail of fire and smoke.

Zell bared his teeth. "Attack!"

All the warlocks turned on Luana and me.

My stomach dropped.

We were outnumbered. This wasn't a battle Luana and I could win. We had to live to fight another day.

Without a second to spare, I brought up my strongest shield and ran to Luana.

I hooked my hand under her arm and helped her up. "Can you run?"

She stared at me. "Run? I want to fight!"

I held her shoulders and stared into her eyes. "I admire your spirit, but we can't win this." I could see the torment in her eyes. As a fighter, she didn't want to give up so easily.

Boom.

The shield was pelted with magic, and cracks spread through it. We had only a couple more seconds before it broke, and we were doomed.

Finally, Luana nodded.

I slipped my hand into hers and led her away from the manor.

It seemed Zell had been right.

Despite my wishes, I was surrendering and walking away.

# 13

LUANA

At first, Keeran and I ran without thinking of where we were going. We just needed to get away from Dark Witch Manor before we were killed.

But with each footfall, the agonizing sensation that we were alone increased and pressed against my chest until it was suffocating.

Gasping for air, I skidded to stop and took a long breath.

Frowning, Keeran turned to me. "Are you all right? What happened?" His eyes skimmed my face, my neck, and my arms. "Are you hurt?"

I shook my head. "I'm fine. I'm just ... lost."

He glanced around the woods. It was still early in the day, but from here, the tall green trees and branches and roots and bushes all looked the same. "I guess we are."

"That's not what I meant."

Keeran's shoulders deflated, as if he had been putting up a show for the last two hours and now he was tired of it. "I know what you mean."

I leaned against a tree trunk, feeling tired myself. "It's just so ... disheartening. We had such clear paths. I was going to take the pack back from Isalia, and you would become a great warlock lord. But just like that—" I snapped my fingers. "—it was all taken from us."

Keeran halted a foot from me, his eyes on mine. "We can't give up. Not yet. We just need to find a safe place to hide while we rethink our strategies."

"I wish I could tell you to go to Unity, but I left that place so Isalia wouldn't find it." I tilted my head. "How about DuMoir Castle?"

Keeran grimaced. "Well, I just had a tense conversation with Thea and Drake the yesterday." He told me about being summoned by the powerful couple to discuss all the problems Keeran and I had been facing. They had learned I was missing and wanted to intervene. Keeran insisted he could do it himself. "Although I would rather try to prove to them we can solve our problems without their help, I'm not so sure we'll succeed now."

"I see your point." If Drake and Thea had cornered me, I would have been on the defensive, and as soon as I walked away, on the offensive. I would probably have done something stupid, like attacking Isalia while injured, and still confident I would win. I shook my head. "So, we won't go to DuMoir Castle."

"But where are we going?" He glanced around, as if he could find a hidden, empty house under the trees.

"I don't know ..."

We needed to hide someplace where Soren and Isalia wouldn't look for us, at least not right away.

As far as I knew, Isalia and her wolves had moved to the Chateau of the Cursed with Soren and his warlocks. We had been kicked out of Dark Witch Manor, and Keeran didn't want to go to DuMoir Castle or the Silverblood estate yet.

Suddenly, his eyes widened. "I think I know where we can go."

<hr>

It took us a little over a day—hiking, running, driving a borrowed car—to get to the Dark Vale pack territory, now abandoned.

When Keeran told me his idea to come back to the place I once had called home, I had been hesitant. But then he explained his warlocks had gone there to look for me and found the place deserted. Which made sense, since Isalia and her wolves were elsewhere.

Unless they had moved again.

Oh well, we would worry about that another time. Right now, I wanted some time to rest and think and breathe.

"Through here." I guided Keeran past the narrow streets that formed my home. He was probably lost since all the houses and streets looked the same. You had to have grown up here, or have werewolf senses, to know where you were going. I halted in front of my house. "This is it."

Keeran frowned, glancing around. "How do you know? They all look alike."

With a small smile, I shook my head and opened the door. To my surprise, the lights still worked, but the place was a mess. Turned couches and tables, ripped curtains, broken portraits and other decorations.

My heart stopped for a second. "By the moon ..."

"What the hell happened here?" Keeran entered the

house, his eyes darting around as if he were looking for danger hidden behind the furniture.

"I'm guessing Isalia searched this place after she kicked me out," I muttered. I picked up a turned table and set it right, though the leg was bent, and now it stood wobbly. "She probably thought I was hiding something she could use against me."

"Were you?" Keeran propped up a chair. Like the table, the chair was damaged.

I picked up a few broken portraits and stared at the pictures. Werewolves were never much into technology, and because of that, we didn't own phones or cameras or computers. These pictures of a young me with my parents were the only ones I had. Tears sprouted to my eyes as I realized that I kept forgetting their faces. In fact, I probably only remember them because of these pictures.

"No," I finally answered. I placed the portraits on the wobbly table. "I wasn't hiding anything."

Keeran let out a long sigh. "Why don't we clean up a little?"

That was so opposite to resting and relaxing and breathing, but there was no way I could sit down and relax in a house that looked like a tornado had ripped through the inside.

I agreed, and we set to work. Keeran worked on the living room and kitchen, while I fixed what I could in the bedrooms and bathrooms—we moved furniture to the right place; pushed broken objects into a corner; swept the floors; changed bedsheets; and put the ripped bedsheets in trash bags, along with any broken decor and shattered glass. After, I raided the nearby houses, which weren't as bad as mine, for food and drinks. From what I'd gathered, I selected our dinner: a box of spaghetti, a can of red sauce and frozen meatballs.

Outside, it was darkening, and Keeran had just finished reorganizing the cabinets with the plates and glasses and pans and pots that hadn't been broken and damaged, when I announced dinner was ready.

Keeran and I sat across the dining table from each other, the plates and food between us. In silence, he served us. And I looked around. From here, I could see the kitchen, the foyer, and the living room, and right now, none of them looked like the familiar place I had grown up.

He placed a full plate in front of me. "Are you okay?"

That was a good question. Was I okay? I had fled from Isalia like a coward again. I had been too hurt to face her properly. I had lost Wyatt and thought he was dead, just to find out he had been bewitched by our enemies. I had considered hiding in Unity and forgetting all of the problems my friends were facing. I was lost and wasn't sure what to do with my life anymore. My home had been vandalized. And, the man in front of me was clueless about what he meant to me.

My appetite gone, I pushed the plate aside. "We need to talk."

Keeran looked at me, mildly curious. "About?"

I opened my mouth, but the words got stuck in my throat. I swallowed them all, took in a deep breath, and tried again. "About us. What we mean to each other."

Keeran balked at my question. "I ... I ..."

"Please, understand, I'm not trying to be pushy," I said quickly. "If you tell me you don't feel anything for me, if you don't want to be with me, I'll understand, and after all of this is over, you can walk away and we'll still be friends. Or not even that ... if you want."

"Luana—"

"Let me finish," I cut him off. If I didn't blurt it all out now, I wasn't sure I could do it later. "But I need you to know something before you walk away. Werewolves usually have mates. They feel their soulmates through what we call a mating bond. It's something like love, but even stronger."

"Like Thea's and Drake's Immortal Vow."

That one was even more powerful since Thea and Drake had chosen each other before they were born, but in some ways, it was the same concept. "Something like that." I held his stare, afraid of his reaction to my next words. "You're my mate, Keeran."

I heard as Keeran's heart skipped a few beats, then sped up. Shock. He was in shock. "Luana, I—"

"I knew I was attracted to you before I felt the bond slipping into place. I think I already loved you before I knew you were my mate, but now ... now I can't help my feelings. I'm in love with you and that isn't going to change. But like I said, I'll respect your feelings, no matter what they are."

I thought about telling him the fact that I would never be able to love another, even if he rejected me, but decided it wasn't worth it. I didn't want him to feel like he had no choice but to be with me. Because he did have a choice. I wouldn't force him to be with me. I wasn't sure how it worked for non-werewolves, but I had my suspicion he wouldn't be able to love another person either.

Slowly, Keeran stood from his chair, walked around the table, and took the chair beside mine. He grabbed my chair and turned it so we were facing each other, our knees touching.

"Luana," he started. I braced myself, trying to get ready for the heartbreak that was sure to follow. He took my hands in his. "I love you, Luana. More than I ever thought I could love someone." I sucked in a sharp breath, sure I heard him wrong. "I love you so much, I wish I could hide you away so you won't get hurt by our enemies."

Tears brimmed in my eyes. "We're in this fight together, Keeran. Isalia is after me, Soren is after you, and now they've joined forces. We need to fight together, even if we risk getting hurt while at it."

"I know. I know. I just wish I could keep you safe, but with your temper, I know I can't." With a small smile, he scooted closer, his long legs flanking mine. "Just promise me you'll be careful."

I stared at him. "Wait, aren't you going to ask me about being my mate? I mean, that's new for me. I can't imagine how you're feeling. A warlock being a werewolf's mate."

Keeran's nose wrinkled. "I think werewolf consort has a better ring to it."

I slapped his shoulder. "Keeran!"

He chuckled. "All right, all right." His eyes grew serious. "I'm not worried about this mate stuff. To be honest, I'm surprisingly okay with it. I love you, you love me, so why not be mates?"

I blinked at him. "You're really okay with it?"

"Let me show you just how okay I am." He clasped my neck and leaned into me. He brushed his lips against mine, and I let out a shuddering breath. "I love you," he whispered.

I scooted to his lap, wrapped my legs around his and my arms around his shoulders, and pressed my mouth against his. Keeran groaned and his hands tightened around my waist. At first, the kiss was slow, but Keeran deepened it and a desperate urge hit me. I needed him, I wanted him, all of him.

As if he could hear my thoughts, Keeran rose from the chair, holding me tight against him, and deposited me on the table, right beside our forgotten, now cold dinner.

A shudder ran through my body as he deepened the kiss more and leaned into me, pressing his hard body against mine. This was it. This was exactly what I wanted.

I skimmed my hands over his back, guiding them down, until they found the hem of his shirt.

A howl pierced my ears. I dropped the shirt and broke the kiss.

"What was that?" Keeran looked to the window, but didn't loosen the hold on me.

The howl came back, louder this time. My chest seized. "It's Wyatt."

# 14

I GLANCED OUT THE LIVING ROOM WINDOW, TRYING TO SEE Wyatt in the darkness, but my eyes weren't like a werewolf's. I couldn't see him hiding in the shadows of the streets, but I knew he was there. All I had to do was keep a line of magic around the house. If he advanced, I would know. I would alert Luana and we would run.

Or fight.

But it had been hours since Wyatt first arrived, and he hadn't done anything. Luana and I had been at a loss why he was here. To attack us? Then why was he standing across the street like a freaking creeper? He could break through the door or the window and come at us.

At some point, Luana had tried going outside to talk to him, but he snarled at her. And when I got closer to try and break the spell over him, Wyatt ran. A few minutes later, he came back, howling and snarling at us.

What was the point in this? Had he been following us since we left Dark Witch Manor? Had Isalia sent him to check on us? Was he like a beacon that would bring the evil she-wolf to us? If that was the plan, then why wasn't she and her wolves and Soren and his warlocks here already?

After a couple of hours of this senseless game, I insisted Luana go to bed. She finally conceded after I agreed we could take turns through the night.

At first, I was fine, but now, sleep was getting to me. Before I ended up dozing off by the window, I went to the kitchen and drank a full glass of cold water. That ought to help with the sleepiness.

On my way back to the living room, I glanced at the dining table, where Luana had told me about the mating bond and I had confessed my love for her.

When she went to bed earlier, I could still see she was worried about the bond, even though I had told her I wasn't.

And I really wasn't. It was a surprise, yes, but honestly, it shouldn't have been. There was no other woman I wanted to spend time with, to talk to, to kiss, or to make love to. There was no other woman who made me feel this will to live, to fight, and this deep desire that I thought I would never experience.

To me, there was Luana. Only Luana.

With my heart full, I dragged a chair to the window and sat down, my gaze trained on the dark street, where Wyatt was hiding.

---

"Keeran."

I shook my head, sending away the fog clouding my mind, and pain shot down my neck. "Freaking ..." I opened my eyes and was startled to find Luana standing in front of me. "What happ—?" The words died when I noticed the light filtering in through the window. Sunlight. It was already daytime. Which meant, I slept through the night, seated in this chair, and that was why my neck was killing me right now. "Shit."

Looking refreshed in dark pants and shirt, Luana crossed her arms. "Why didn't you wake me up? I thought we would switch at least once in the middle of the night."

I rolled my shoulders and groaned. "That was the plan, but I guess I fell asleep without meaning to." A sudden thought filled my mind, and I shot up from the chair. Pain ricocheted down my back. "Where's Wyatt?"

Luana stepped behind me and pulled me back. I plopped down on the chair and her hands flew to my neck. "I don't know. My guess is that he left in the middle of the night." She started massaging my neck and shoulders, and instant relief flooded my senses. "And I'm assuming he went back to tell Isalia and Soren where we are."

I rose to my feet and faced her. "Then we need to leave."

She nodded. "I agree, but I don't think we need to hurry." She grabbed my hand and pulled me down on the chair again. Her delicate hands found my neck once more. "Before we flee, we should talk about our plans. Where to go, what to do, who to kill." I felt her flinch, even if I hadn't seen it. She let out a long sigh. "If we rush off without a firm plan, chances are we'll get caught again and end up in a worse situation."

"You're right," I muttered. Although, to be honest, I had no idea how we would accomplish anything.

There was too much going on, and it was so freaking confusing. Farrah had left to help her brother. Soren and Isalia had joined forces and were after Luana and me. Wyatt had been spelled by Soren, I assumed. And Zell and the other warlocks had turned against me.

Was I still the warlock lord, or had that title been taken from me too? Not that it mattered. I didn't care about being the warlock lord. What I cared about was finding my mother and finding a place I could belong. I thought that was with the warlocks at Dark Witch Manor, but now, I wasn't so sure.

Now, I was starting to think I belonged someplace else.

To someone else.

I glanced at Luana from over my shoulder. She was so incredibly beautiful and strong and hardheaded, and I loved her the way she was.

"What?" she snapped. She pressed her finger to my cheek and pushed my head forward again. "If you keep bothering me, I won't massage your neck."

She had trusted me last night and told me about the mating bond. Even though she feared I would reject her, she told me that I was her mate.

And now it was my turn to tell her something.

"There's more to the prophecy," I whispered.

Her hands stilled. "What do you mean?"

"Zell told me that there's more to the prophecy," I said, my voice clearer. "When I kill my father, I'll turn evil." She didn't say anything, and I wondered if she was praying to the mating gods to undo our bond right now. "Did you hear me?"

"Yes," she answered, her tone soft.

"Aren't you worried? Your mate will turn evil." The odd thing was, until now, I had been worried about me. Of course, I didn't want to turn evil, but now my worry had shifted to Luana. I was afraid I would turn evil and hurt her.

She stepped around me and sat down on my lap. "I don't believe you'll turn evil." She truly believed that. I could see it in her eyes. I could hear it in her voice, but that didn't change the truth.

"I was told these prophecies are never wrong."

A small line marred her forehead. "Sometimes, we need to believe in the impossible. Maybe there's another part of the prophecy we don't know. Maybe you'll turn evil for five seconds, then the goodness in you—" She pressed her palm against my heart. "—will win."

"I wish it was that simple."

"What other choice do we have? Hide? If we do that, then we'll be allowing Isalia and Soren to spread their viciousness throughout the world. They will kill more witches and werewolves and supernaturals until someone stands up to them. Besides, I'm sure you know they won't stop looking for us."

I hated when she was right. "So you're saying I should accept being evil?"

"No, of course not. Just ... keep an open mind. Anything can happen. And I'll be there, no matter what. If you turn evil, I'll lock you up somehow and—"

"That's reassuring."

"—and find a way to bring you back." She stared into my eyes, not one sliver of doubt in her gaze. "You trust me, don't you?"

I wound my arms around her and pulled her to me. "Wholeheartedly." She buried her face in my neck, and I wished we could stay like this forever. No, not like this. I wish I could take her to bed and forget everything else but making love to her forever. "So, what do we do now?"

She pulled back and looked at me again. "We're only two now, against too many. Our only chance is to get Soren and Isalia alone. Preferably one by one. If we fight them without their lackeys, we have a chance of winning." She paused. "If I defeat Isalia, the pack will be free of her terrible hold."

"And if I kill Soren, Wyatt will be free of the enchantment, and the witches will be safe." I frowned. "I don't even care about the warlock coven anymore. Zell can keep it and become the warlock lord. All I want is peace."

A soft smile tugged the corner of her lips. "You sound like Drake and Thea."

I snorted. "They might have rubbed off on me."

"Well, that's not a bad thing."

I knew it wasn't, but I was still resentful of their lack of trust in me. I wanted to prove to them that I could do it, that Luana and I could do it. "Still, how do we lure Soren and Isalia out?"

"If we show up at the chateau, they will send the warlocks and werewolves at us, and we won't have an opportunity to fight them alone." Luana thought for a second. "I think we need help for this."

"We don't have anyone."

Her smile widened a bit. "I have an idea."

---

WE DIDN'T LEAVE RIGHT AWAY. FIRST, WE ATE BREAKFAST, THEN packed for our trip. As usual, we didn't know how long we would be gone or where we would end up, so we packed the essentials—a few toiletries and a change of clothes. A thick cloak too, since summer had officially ended and the air was becoming crisper, especially at night.

At least Luana seemed a little bit less tense now that she had some of her clothes back—even if she was still dressed in black leather pants and a shirt.

Back in the woods, I used my magic and did a tracking spell on Farrah. I didn't have anything of hers, so the spell was weak, but it would guide us in the direction she had gone. At least, that was how it was supposed to work in theory, and I hoped it worked, because I had no idea where she had gone.

Luana and I followed the invisible line the spell had created, going down a wide valley, then around a mountain. The only thing I knew was that we were the farthest from DuMoir Castle I had ever been.

We crossed a shallow creek, and a few yards from a cliff's edge, the spell died.

I halted. "This cursed magic ..."

"What happened?" Luana asked, stopping by my side.

I closed my eyes and focused, trying to cast the spell again. I felt the flicker of the magic, the energy taking shape, but it didn't last. "It's like there's a barrier here. The spell won't hold anymore."

Luana looked around. "A barrier?"

I shrugged. "Yeah, like a protection."

"Which means we're close."

"If not from the fae, then a witch coven," I said. That, or my magic was still unstable and couldn't even hold a tracking spell anymore. Which shouldn't be the case since I was feeling well, and even though my magic was far from being where I wanted, I had better control over it now.

"Let's hope it's the fae."

Not that it was much better. As far as I knew, the fae didn't like any other supernaturals—much less humans. Focusing again, I sent a blast of magic out. A few feet from us, my magic faded. "It's not like when I create shields and the magic hits it. Whatever this is, the magic just ... vanishes."

"Then it must be the fae, which means we're going in the right direction." Luana raised her chin and sniffed the air. "I can definitely feel something different in the air. Let's keep going."

Luana took a step forward, but I caught her arm and held her back. "What if whatever this is—" I gestured to the cliff in front of us. "—is some kind of booby trap?"

Frowning, Luana crouched and picked up a small pebble in her hand. She straightened and threw it toward the cliff.

Not ten yards from us, the pebble disappeared, and the air around seemed to tremble. "It is some kind of shield." She slipped her hand in mine. "Let's go."

I channeled my magic, keeping it inside my veins, ready for anything.

Ten steps later, the air around us shimmered and everything changed. Surprised, I let go of my magic as I took in the area. The cliff was gone, replaced by a clearing surrounded by a tree-covered hill. The clearing was filled with large tents, and among the tents, fae dressed in full silver-plated battle armor milled about.

Realizing they weren't alone, Daleigh stepped away from the group and marched toward us.

The man pointed his silver spear at us. "You're not welcome here."

"Daleigh, we would like to talk to Farrah, please," I said, my tone as diplomatic as I could muster.

"She's busy." He gestured to his people. "As you can see, we're all busy. Leave before I call my guards."

Luana clenched her fists. "Hear me out, pretty boy. I'm not—"

"Daleigh?" It was Farrah's voice. I glanced over Daleigh's shoulder and spotted the young woman, also dressed in similar silver armor, walking toward us. Her blue gaze met mine and she frowned. "Keeran? Luana? What's going on?"

"They were just leaving," Daleigh barked.

"No, we weren't," Luana snarled.

Farrah halted beside her brother. "What happened?" She looked side to side. "Where's Wyatt?"

Luana's shoulders deflated. "By the moon, there's so much you don't know."

Farrah's eyes widened. "What don't I know?"

Luana and I filled her in on all that had happened after she left Dark Witch Manor. Luana told her about hers and Wyatt's capture, their torture, and her escape from the Chateau of the Cursed. Luana didn't mention Wyatt's current situation, though I was sure she would soon. She also didn't tell Farrah about Unity, because there were too many ears close by.

Then it was my turn. I told Farrah about my desperate attempt to find Luana and Wyatt, and the betrayal from Zell and the other warlocks. Like Luana, I also omitted certain information from Farrah, like the part of the prophecy that said I would become as evil as my father if I killed him.

Just rehashing everything now made me extremely tired and depressed. Had it all been a couple of weeks ago, and not three years? Because it felt like much more.

"We're planning on going to the Chateau of the Cursed and drawing Soren and Isalia out," I said. "But we need help."

Farrah seemed to consider it. "What kind of help?"

"You can't be really considering this!" Daleigh shouted. "We need you he—"

"What kind of help?" Farrah asked again, cutting her brother off. His fair skin grew red with rage.

"To end this, we need to kill both Soren and Isalia," I told her. "But we can't do it with all their lackeys around them. We need you and your magic to help us draw them to us. Alone."

Farrah's brows furrowed. "If I can get close enough, I can create an illusion. Make them believe there's a need to get out of whatever place they are hiding and come to us."

Luana's eyes widened. "You can do that?"

"It's tricky, but it can be done," Farrah said.

"Farrah!" Daleigh said, his tone low but firm. "We need you here. I need you here."

She turned her icy eyes to her brother. "You and I know this damn fight is useless. I've done all I can for you here!"

He narrowed his eyes at her. "I know this fight is useless, but unless they stop, we won't either. And you're the strongest one here. We need you so we can show them we won't back off."

"I won't hurt innocents!" she snapped.

He stared at her. "You know I wouldn't either, but that's beyond us right now. All I want is for us to—" He pressed his lips tight. "Please, Farrah. We allowed you back."

"And I'll be forever thankful for that." She clasped his hands in hers. "But you have to understand. When you needed me, I came to help you; now they need me, and I want to help."

His blue eyes were pained. "I just got you back."

She leaned into him and he met her halfway. They rested their foreheads together. "I'll be back as soon as I can. I promise."

He held on to her hands. "Please, Farrah …"

She pressed a kiss to his forehead and said something in a strange language. During the short sentence, her voice gained a lyrical tone, as if she was almost singing. Was that their mother language?

Farrah turned to us. "Let's go."

Luana was ready and marched out of the camp with Farrah, but I lagged a few seconds behind. She was going, just like that? Without changing or without gathering any supplies?

As Farrah marched through the shield and disappeared right before my eyes, Daleigh let out a pained sigh.

"I'm sorry," I muttered, not sure what else to say.

He glared at me. "Just go before I change my mind and kill you."

I frowned, wishing I had something more to say, something to appease him, to bring him comfort, but I barely knew the guy. I didn't really have anything to say to him.

I tipped my chin, in farewell, and followed the girls.

**15**

---



AFTER WE LEFT THE FAE CAMP, WE MARCHED STRAIGHT TOWARD the Chateau of the Cursed. All the while, Farrah was mostly quietly. She only spoke in two situations: when Keeran asked her why the fae were fighting, and she answered that her group had found other fae from an enemy court and they attacked first, and when we talked about our plan.

"You say they are inside this chateau place," she said, her silver brows curled down. "I think it'll be hard to draw just Isalia and Soren out. It might be a better option to draw their werewolves and warlocks out, then you two sneak in."

"We're concerned that we would be trapped inside, if the lackeys came back early," Keeran said.

"Or if most of them didn't leave," I added.

"That is a risk." Farrah waved her hand and the low branch in her way turned white and bent up. Once we were all past it, the branch fell back in place, and the ice covering it melted. "But I can't think of why Soren and Isalia would leave the chateau without at least a couple of their lackeys."

"True," I muttered. "I kn—"

I halted, my body tense.

Keeran frowned at me. "What is it?"

I found Farrah's gaze. "It's Wyatt."

Her blue eyes rounded. "Here?"

"He's a few yards away, hiding," I said, voice low, but Wyatt probably heard me anyway.

He snarled low. A warning.

"Tell me where he is," Farrah said.

Farrah and Wyatt had shared a connection since they had first met. Maybe because they were young and had been thrust into dangerous situations. They had to grow up fast, and some of it had been together. Even though they hadn't known each other long, they had been through a lot together.

If one person could get through to Wyatt, it was Farrah. I was sure of it. "Fifty yards southwest."

She didn't even blink before zipping through the trees toward Wyatt. I cursed under my breath and followed her. I wouldn't interfere, but I wanted to be close in case I needed to.

"Wyatt," she whispered, slowing down.

Like before, Wyatt looked more like a wild wolf than a werewolf capable of thinking and reasoning. His fur was dirty, his eyes red, and there was foam at the corner of his mouth. Eyes set on Farrah, he lowered his head and snarled, his razor-sharp teeth showing.

Then, he spun around and took off.

---

As we resumed our way to the Chateau of the Cursed, I could see that the brief Wyatt sighting had affected Farrah.

She was even quieter now, a little slower, her head down, and she didn't use her magic to move obstacles out of her way.

I was a little worried about how that would affect the upcoming battle. Hopefully, her mindset would match her intricate silver armor, and she would kick ass with us.

I was trying not to think that Wyatt had spotted us coming this way and had probably already reported to Soren and Isalia when we arrived in Chateau of the Cursed territory.

The times I had been here before, I had been brought in and carried out while unconscious, so I hadn't seen the place.

The outside was as creepy and ugly as the inside. The forest was dark here, as if it knew that evil lurked, the trees thin and frail, the grass mostly gone, leaving behind only dried dirt and broken twigs. Hidden among it all was a fort-like building with tall, gray stone walls and only a few narrow windows.

"Are you freaking kidding me?" Keeran muttered. "How are we supposed to get in there?"

"They will have to exit somewhere," Farrah said. "I'll draw them out, away from the chateau, and you guys sneak inside." She glanced at the both of us. "Ready?"

Keeran slipped his hand in mine and tugged me closer. "Be careful."

I held on to his hand. "You too." I rose on tiptoes and pressed my lips to his. I didn't want to think we were about to face our biggest enemies—alone! "I'll find you as soon as I'm done."

He nodded, then he glanced at Farrah. "We're ready."

Farrah closed her eyes and called her magic. A chilly breeze rushed around us and Farrah's long silver hair floated behind her back as if she were underwater. Slowly, she raised her arms, her fingers white, almost like they had turned into snow themselves.

I heard them before I saw them. The deep growls of monsters in the distance, crushing through the forest. I turned my head, following their sounds. From here, we couldn't see much, just the top of the ice monsters' heads above the trees' crowns, and the icy swirl dancing around them.

They threw ice shards and snowballs at the fort-like building. At first, I wondered what a snowball could do, but I had severely underestimated Farrah. The snowballs were probably the size of cars, and they shook the walls of the fort with each hit.

"Wow," Keeran said, his eyes wide.

"It really is impressive."

With her eyes still closed, Farrah said, "They are coming."

Not even five seconds later, the main gates opened. Warlocks and werewolves rushed out, attacking the ice monsters with all they had.

Still controlling them, Farrah made the monsters attack too, but retreat at the same time, in order to draw our enemies out. It worked, and soon warlocks and werewolves were chasing after the ice monsters through the forest.

"It's time," Keeran said.

Farrah opened her eyes. "I don't think all their lackeys left, but there might be only a few left inside."

"We can deal with a few," I said, holding on to the little confidence inside me.

This was it.

This was the end.

We would face Soren and Isalia now. We would defeat them and start a new chapter in our lives.

"Here," Keeran said. He waved his hand around us. "I've cast a weak cloaking spell. It should give us cover while sneaking in." He gestured toward the fort. "Let's go."

The three of us rushed toward the gates, and even though I knew we had the cloaking spell in place, I still ducked every time I heard a noise or saw someone's shadows.

A small courtyard greeted us inside the gates before the tall doors to the chateau. Slowly, we walked inside.

And found it deserted.

Keeran closed his eyes for a moment. "I feel ... I feel Soren's magic this way." He pointed up the stairs.

I inhaled deeply, but Isalia's scent was everywhere and it was easy to detect. "I know where Isalia is."

Keeran glanced at me. "See you soon."

He ran up the stairs and I stared at him for a moment.

Farrah tugged my arm. "We don't have much time. I don't know how long I can keep the ice warriors up from here. Let's go."

I nodded and sniffed the air again. I followed Isalia's scent down the hallway, past the stairs, to the back of the chateau. We found a large area that resembled a sunroom, though here the windows were tall but narrow. Weak sunlight streamed through, illuminating the rough gray floor and the sleek black leather couches.

However, Isalia wasn't here.

Another she-wolf was.

Bleiz, Isalia's right hand since she started this crazy quest, smiled at me. "Hello, Luana. Long time no see."

I clenched my hands. "Where's Isalia?"

Bleiz opened her arms. "Not here, as you can see."

Then, what did it mean? Had Wyatt really warned them we were coming? So, this was all a trap?

"We were tricked," I whispered. Fear gripped my chest.

Bleiz smiled, her fangs elongating. "You think?"

She turned in two seconds flat and jumped at me.

I started to shift, but Farrah was faster. She produced an ice spear and threw it. The spear pierced through the wolf's chest. The wolf whimpered before falling hard on the ground. She shuddered as she shifted back to her human form and blood spread around her.

I gulped. "Remind me to always be on your side."

Farrah let out a hollow chuckle. "Will do."

I stared at Farrah. "If this was a trap, then Keeran is also in danger." And I was sure being trapped in a room with only one wolf wasn't the main attraction. There was more danger coming. "We need to find him and get out."

## 16

I FOLLOWED SOREN'S MAGIC SIGNATURE TO THE SECOND FLOOR of the chateau. I found the room that looked like his office and another one that looked like his suite, but there was no sign of Soren anywhere.

There was no one.

My gut dropped.

This was a freaking trap.

I turned to leave, and ten warlocks entered the suite and surrounded me. A bitter taste stained my tongue as I recognized the warlocks—they had been at Dark Witch Manor, pretending to be my peers, before fleeing with my father.

I channeled my power, but worry laced my muscles. There was only so much I could do against ten warlocks.

"Surrender," Eliphaz said. "Lord Soren would be really mad at us if we hurt you."

I snorted. "You'll have to kill me to make me surrender."

Black flames appeared in his hands. "So be it."

He threw the flames at me. I waved my hands, redirecting them outward and toward the other warlocks. That bought me a couple of seconds, but they recovered and sent bolts at me.

I felt like a monkey in a cage as I jumped, danced, and twisted out of the way, trying to avoid all the hits sent in my direction. I heard the sizzle as the bolts grazed my clothes and burned holes in them.

Eventually, I brought up a shield, but against an arc of ten warlocks, I knew the magical wall wouldn't last long.

Eliphaz offered me a sly grin before extending his hand before him. The black flames became bluish shadows. Crackling came from the shadows, and soon they turned into lightning.

He threw that ray of electricity out. The shield practically melted away.

I ducked and threw one of my bolts at him, but he burned through it with another electrical ray.

Then one of his hits struck me in the chest, like electricity. I trembled with the shock and pain coursing through my body. Eliphaz took advantage of that moment. He cast tight magical bindings around my wrists and chests. I groaned, trying to break it, but before I could make it budge, the other warlocks sent their magic to the bindings, making the stronger.

"And just because it's fun." Eliphaz sent another bolt to me. It hit the same place as the previous one, but this time it hurt more. I fell on my knees, fighting the black spots that crowded my vision. "Bring him out."

Hands took hold of my arms and I was dragged out of the room. I tried paying attention to where I was being taken, but my mind swam as the pain pulsed through my muscles, causing them to spasm.

I was thrown against the rough floor, my shoulder hitting

the ground, and I bit back a scream. I wouldn't give them the satisfaction of seeing me in pain.

I blinked, pushing back some of the darkness from my sight. Eliphaz withdrew the bindings from around me before closing a heavy wooden door. He looked at me through the small rectangle at the top half. "Lord Soren will be pleased."

"Keeran?"

Luana's voice sent a jolt of fear through my chest. Pain forgotten, I pushed to my feet and spied through the window above the door. "Luana?" She was in the cell across from me, watching me like I was watching her. "What happened?"

"I was a trap," she said. "They caught us as we were searching for you."

I glanced around, but couldn't see much from here. "Where's Farrah?"

The young fae showed her face through the door window of the cell next to Luana's. "I'm here."

"I'm sorry for bringing you into this," I said.

Eliphaz let out a loud, evil cackle. "I'm not sorry." He glanced at the other warlocks. "Are you guys sorry? In fact, we're enjoying this a lot. We've got our lord's son, and two pretty women." He grinned at me. "You know, it has been a while since I've touched a woman. Since it's going to take a while for Lord Soren to get here, I say we enjoy ourselves." He winked at the others. "What do you think?"

The warlocks uttered their eloquent agreement.

"You can't be serious," I said, appalled he was even considering something so evil. But then again, he had been on Soren's side when my father kept witches locked in dungeons to serve as sex slaves and procreators. Fear filled my veins. I felt an anxiety attack taking shape. "Keep away from them."

As if he hadn't heard me, Eliphaz turned to Luana's cell. He cast on her the same binding spell he had on me, then opened her door. "I'm going to enjoy this."

Rage flow inside me and red tinted my vision.

I lost it.

I threw out my hands and my power exploded from my palms. Red waves of magic flowed forward, shattering the wooden door into a million pieces. The magic kept going and going, taking every ounce of my energy from me. The red wave rolled across the hallway and into the other cells. I heard screams and yelps and the rush of people as they ran, trying to get away from the blast.

But they couldn't.

My rage, my anger was imbued in my power, and right now, it was limitless.

"Keeran!" a voice called. I knew this voice. "Keeran, please, stop!" I was sure that voice was important. "Stop, now!" I blinked. Wait a minute ...

I reigned my magic in. Slowly, it faded and I fell on my knees, my breath shallow—I felt like I had run a marathon.

"What ...?" I shook my head, but that only made me dizzier.

Luana knelt in front of me, her hands on my face. "Keeran, are you okay?"

I searched her eyes. "What happened?" Farrah walked into the cell, holding her hand over her mouth and nose. Why? "What's going on?"

Then it hit me.

We were in a dungeon underneath the Chateau of the Cursed. Soren's warlocks had threatened to rape of Luana and Farrah.

And I lost it.

I let out all of my power and—

I glanced at Luana's shoulder and saw the legs and arms peeking out from the hallway.

"Holy shit," I muttered as another string of curses rose to my throat.

Luana pulled on my face, forcing me to look at her again. "It's okay." Why did she say it was okay with her eyes full of unshed tears? "You did what you had to do."

"I didn't I hurt you?" I asked, looking from Luana to Farrah.

Farrah shrugged. "Even on a subconscious level, I guess you knew what you were doing and you didn't want to hurt us."

"It doesn't make sense." How could I hurt so many people and still know what I was doing? Was I this evil?

Hopefully, not yet.

Luana tugged on my arms. "Come on. We don't know when the others are coming back. We should go."

I unfolded to my feet. My head swam, but I fought against it, not willing to show any kind of weakness right now, not after the atrocity I had committed.

However, even though I knew I had killed all the warlocks, I hadn't been prepared for when we left the cell. There were twisted bodies and blood everywhere. And the smell ... it wasn't a rotten scent, since they had just been killed, but it was a pungent and unpleasant smell neverthe-less. It turned my stomach.

Feeling depleted, I didn't cast another cloaking spell over us as we rushed out of the chateau, but thankfully, we didn't encounter anyone. From Farrah's reports, she had let go of her ice monsters the moment we hit the forest, and the warlocks and wolves who had been fighting the monsters were now rushing back to the chateau.

Without wasting a second, we marched on, putting some distance between them and us.

We had been running through the forest for almost an hour, when Luana halted. "I can smell something," she said, her sight straining against the green vegetation surrounding us. "A person and blood."

"Blood?" I asked, already channeling more of my magic in case we needed to fight.

"Wait." Luana raised her hand. She sniffed the air. "We know this person." She suddenly rushed forward.

I cursed and followed her, Farrah a few feet behind me.

Not a minute later, Luana slowed down.

I quickly caught up with her and followed her line of sight. Only a few yards away, a warlock crawled out from behind some bushes, his arms and face smeared with blood.

"Galroth!" I knelt in front of him and reached for him. "What happened?"

The warlock gripped my arms tight, his hands shaking hard, and his wide eyes found mine. "You have to come," he rasped, his voice barely a whisper. "Zell asked for you."

Luana snorted. "For what?"

"It's Soren," Galroth continued.

My gut tightened. "What did Soren do?"

"Dark Witch Manor." He swallowed hard, as if even that hurt. "Soren is attacking Dark Witch Manor."

# 17

I COULD SEE THE ANGUISH IN KEERAN'S FACE AS GALROTH DIED in his arms—despite everything Zell had done to him, to us, he wanted to go help him.

That was how good of a man Keeran was.

And he thought he could simply turn evil after killing his father.

Not that it was impossible, of course, but he had such a good heart.

Although, he had scared me when Eliphaz had threatened to take Farrah and me. He had lost control and drowned in rage. He hadn't been evil, not really, but it was easy to see how the evil could get ahold of that rage and turn it into something worse.

Perhaps we should be afraid of him becoming a monster like his father, but I knew his heart better than that.

"You aren't considering it, are you?" Farrah asked. Like me, Farrah already knew this side of Keeran and knew what he was thinking. "They tried to kill you both and you want to help them?"

Keeran gently laid Galroth's body on the ground. Then, he stood tall and faced us. "This is where we differ from all of them. We do what it's right, even when they don't." His jaw ticked. He was still struggling with his choice, but he wouldn't show it to us. "If you two don't want to go, I understand. But I'm going."

Farrah humphed, and I had to swallow a growl that rose in my throat. Unlike Keeran, I was still divided. Yes, I liked to think I was a good woman at heart, but enough was enough. Zell had tried to kill us.

"Keeran—"

"You heard Galroth," he said, cutting me off. "Zell asked him to come find me. He wouldn't have done that if it wasn't important."

The only thing I could think was that Zell wanted Keeran there so he could be killed by his father. But then Zell would be left alone with his warlocks to face Soren. It didn't make much sense.

Farrah let out a low groan. "Wyatt must be there, right?"

Shit, I had forgotten about that. With Soren in command of Wyatt's actions, it was probable that the poor werewolf was killing people against his will. He had no idea what he was doing.

"All right, I'll go," I said. "For Wyatt, but I want to get him out of there without getting further involved."

"What if the fight comes to you?" Keeran asked.

I raised my chin. "Then I'll do my best to defend myself."

He narrowed his eyes at me. For all my tough talk, he knew, just as much as I did, that it wouldn't be that simple. The moment I laid eyes on the fight, I would pick a side and help.

And that was exactly what happened when we got to

Dark Witch Manor. Hell had broken loose in the mansion's backyard, and the orchard was half destroyed as warlocks fought against warlocks and werewolves. Despite all the magic these men possessed, Isalia's she-wolves were still deadly.

"I don't see Wyatt," Farrah said.

From our spot at the edge of the forest, we could see everything—the spells that zipped through the air, the trees that exploded with either magic, the wolves who showed off their bloody teeth. We saw it all—except the young wolf and our two main enemies.

I inhaled deeply, trying to locate Wyatt's scent among the chaos, but it was too hard to pick up on his scent. All I smelled was blood and sweat and burnt leaves and trees. "I can't find him either."

Farrah turned huge eyes to me. "So he isn't here?"

"I wouldn't say that," Keeran said, his gaze trained on the battlefield. "We just haven't found him yet." He walked out of our hiding spot. "Come on."

He sprinted forward. An urge to hold him back hit me, almost as strong as the urge to run into the fight and rip everyone apart, no matter what side they were on. I was so tired of fighting.

Farrah and I followed Keeran. He joined the fray and found Flavius, one of the warlocks who had helped him the most during his brief stay as the warlock lord.

"Keeran!" Flavius exclaimed, genuinely glad. "You're here!" He clasped Keeran's shoulders with his bloody hands. "I wasn't sure you would come, or if Galroth would find you."

Keeran put his hand over Flavius's. "I'm here. Tell me what to do."

Flavius's eyes gained a saddened glint. "We're losing. Bad."

I looked at the fight. We stood with Flavius at the back of the warlock side, from where he mostly orchestrated the battle. Zell's warlocks kept shields up, trying to evade the spells from Soren's warlocks, while firing every moment they got a chance, but shields weren't effective against werewolves. Isalia's she-wolves advanced on the warlocks and ripped through them as if they were paper dolls.

"Where's Zell?" Keeran asked. "And Soren?"

"Where's Wyatt?" Farrah asked.

"Where's Isalia?" I asked.

Flavius shook his head once. "I'm not sure. Zell went inside to retrieve something, but I haven't seen him since. We're just trying to hold the line."

A spell zipped past us, inches from my head. My heart jumped to my throat. "What the ...?"

"Sorry." Stepping forward, Flavius threw his hand out. Another shield appeared between the two groups. "It won't last long. It never does."

A flash of light at the corner of my eyes caught my attention. I glanced to the mansion besides us. The lights flashed again. No, not lights. Spells.

"There." I pointed to the tall windows on the east side of the first floor. "That's Soren."

"I bet Isalia is with him," Keeran said.

"And Wyatt," Farrah added.

Keeran's eyes found mine. "Are you ready?"

Ready to do what we couldn't do at the Chateau of the Cursed. Take out Soren and Isalia and end this terrible war for once and for all.

I nodded. "Yes."

The three of us sneaked into the mansion. Warlocks and werewolves were fighting everywhere, and we had to stop to either clear the way, or help, a dozen times before we reached the throne room.

My steps faltered in the doorway.

Inside, Zell and a handful of warlocks battled against Soren and Isalia, in her wolf form, and two of her she-wolves. And behind them all was Wyatt, ready to attack.

The moment I made up my mind and advanced, Soren sent a wave of black magic that washed out over Zell and his warlocks. The men fell on the ground, writhing.

"No!" Keeran shouted. He ran toward the warlocks, but Isalia's she-wolves jumped him.

I shifted, ruining yet another set of clothes, and advanced on the poor she-wolves who dared touch my mate.

Noticing they were coming for him, Keeran brought up a shield and one of the she-wolves bounced off it. The other was smart and ran in a wide arc, but I jumped her before she could reach Keeran.

I bit down on her throat, urging her to surrender. But she didn't. In fact, she tried attacking me as if I hadn't been holding her down. I pressed down with all the strength I had and her neck snapped.

Letting go of her limp body, I stomped my foot on the hard floor and snarled at Isalia.

She snarled back at me.

Soren let out an amused chuckle. "Now, that's entertaining."

Standing beside a wobbly Zell, Keeran glared at his father. "Entertaining? You know you sound mad?"

Soren laughed again. "My dear son, I'm completely fine." Two snakes of shadowy smoke sprouted from his hands and curled up his arms. "I'm more than fine. I'm perfect."

"Kill him," Zell croaked. "K-Keeran, you've got to kill him."

In the blink of an eye, Soren pointed at Zell, and the black snake zoomed through the air like lightning, hitting him in the chest. Zell's eyes widened, his face paled, his body trembled as he slipped down.

"No!" Keeran shouted as he helped the other warlock to the ground.

"K-kill him," Zell tried again, his voice too thin for Keeran to hear. In his chest, his heart spiked, too fast to be sustained.

Keeran shot up and sent a strike of red magic toward Soren. But Soren wasn't an idiot. He knew Keeran would attack him, so he brought up a shield. Keeran's spell hit the shield and faded away.

"You think you can defeat me?" Soren asked, taunting Keeran. "You got a lot of practicing to do, boy. It's a shame you won't have time for that." The snakes from Soren's arms zoomed around the room, as fast as before. They left a trail of fire behind them as they circled around us, meeting each other on the other side.

The fire instantly billowed upward, enclosing the room.

Farrah, who had been trying to reach Wyatt unnoticed, jumped back. She retreated, meeting us in the center of the fire ring.

"You coward!" Keeran shouted. "Face me, man to man."

Soren's evil laughter echoed through the room. "It doesn't matter how I win, my son. As long as I win."

He lifted his arms high, and the fire grew even more, reaching the ceiling. We couldn't see or hear anything past the fire.

I shifted back into my human body and glanced around. "What now?"

But Keeran didn't hear me. He was kneeling beside Zell, holding the hand of the warlock. "I'm here."

Zell blinked. "I can't see you." His heartbeat slowed. Zell was dying, and I didn't think there was anything we could do to save him now. "But I can hear you."

"I'm sorry," Keeran whispered.

Zell shook his head. "N-no, I'm sorry."

A cloak appeared over my shoulders and I jumped. Farrah had grabbed the cloak from one of the fallen warlocks and covered my naked body. I mouthed a "thank you" at her.

"It's okay," Keeran said.

"No, i-it's not okay," Zell said, his voice failing. "You were our rightful leader. I should've trusted you, guided you, helped you. F-followed you." Zell reached one of his trembling hands to Keeran's face. "Don't give up. You'll be a great leader someday."

I heard as Zell's heart slowed and slowed, until his hands fell, his head drooped, and his body went limp.

"Zell?" Keeran shook the warlock's shoulders. "Zell?"

The fire around us advanced, closing the circle. Sparks crackled left and right, sending my nerves through the roof. "We need to leave now!" I grabbed Keeran's hand and tugged him up. When his eyes met mine, I said, "If we don't do something, we'll be burned alive. Can you do a spell?"

He let go of me and looked down at his hands, as if seeing them for the first time. Losing Zell in such a horrid way had snapped his mind.

Keeran was in shock again.

"I think I can break through the fire," Farrah said. She opened her arms wide, and a chilly air swirled around us.

The invisible magic slammed into the fire wall, sending more sparks everywhere. As if sensing its integrity was threatened, the circle closed in on us more.

"Farrah!"

She joined her hands and ice crawled from the ground up the fire, in a thin line. Groaning, Farrah opened her arms again, and the thin line broke in half, pushing the fire back and creating a doorway for us.

"Let's go!" she yelled before jumping through the passage.

Not trusting Keeran's actions right now, I grabbed his hand and pulled him with me.

We exited a bad situation, but encountered another one. The fire had spread everywhere. The furniture, the curtains, the walls. It consumed most of the throne room and had already spread down the hallways.

Soren and Isalia were long gone.

Just as the thought entered my mind, Farrah turned huge eyes to me. "Where's Wyatt?"

## 18

SOMETHING CLICKED IN THE NUMBNESS OF MY MIND.

"Wyatt?" I asked, feeling as if I had emerged from a dark ocean. Zell might not have been a friend, but he hadn't been an evil warlock either. He had been a mentor, and I had just lost him. I wouldn't lose anyone else today, not if I could help it. "Didn't he leave with Soren and Isalia?"

"There's no way to be sure," Farrah said.

A cracking sound echoed through the room, followed by the boom of something heavy falling on the hard floor. The fire sparked higher and wider.

"I think …" Luana closed her eyes and inhaled deeply. "I think I can smell him." She coughed. "It's hard to say with all the smoke."

This cursed smoke and the fire. Any action was getting too hard with the smoke and the fire. To see, to move, and to breathe. We needed to get away from here. But not before we found Wyatt. "Where?"

Luana inhaled deeply again. "I can't—" A fit of cough assaulted her.

"I can try something," Farrah said. She pushed her arms outward. That chilly air that always accompanied her magic danced around us, and advanced over the fire. Her ice magic pushed the fire and the smoke back a little, giving us more room. "Can you find him now?"

"I can try," Luana said.

"Then be quick," Farrah urged. "This won't last long, and the fire will come back with a vengeance."

Luana tried again. She pointed to a corner of the room. "There."

Dodging the fire and the destroyed furniture, we rushed to where Luana had pointed. Just as she had predicted, Wyatt was behind a half-burned column, still in his wolf form.

"Wyatt!" Farrah called.

Luana shook his head. "His heart is slow and his breathing even worse. He won't wake up unless we get him out of here."

Wolf Wyatt was huge, but I didn't care. I called my magic to give me strength and picked him up in my arms. "Let's go."

We turned to leave, but the fire Farrah had pushed back returned, and like she said, it seemed stronger and wilder than before. We were trapped on this side of the room.

"I can't keep pushing the fire back," Farrah said. "It's a magical fire so it takes too much of me, and if I try, we'll be trapped in the middle of the mansion with not only Wyatt passed out, but me too."

The heat and smoked pressed into us and we coughed some more. Even if we stayed low and covered our faces to avoid smoke inhalation, we would all pass out soon.

Holding on to Wyatt, I looked around. A few yards behind us, thick curtains burned to a crisp.

"The window," I said.

Farrah didn't waste time. She called her magic and pushed back the fire in front of the window and on the curtains. Farrah held on to her magic as Luana rushed forward and opened the window. The fire roared toward us, toward the window with renewed strength, but Farrah's ice kept it back.

"It should be okay." Luana sat on the windowsill and looked down. We were on the first floor, but the entire mansion was elevated. "Come on." She grabbed Farrah's hand and helped her out first. She gestured for me to go next.

I shook my head. "You go first and be ready to catch Wyatt in case I lose my balance."

She gave me a quick nod and jumped out.

Then, I sat on the windowsill and looked down. Without a doubt, this freaking jump was nothing for a werewolf or a fae, and it would have been okay for a warlock who wasn't carrying a half-dead wolf in his arms.

Heat licked my back and the roar of fire crackled in my ears.

I jumped.

Luana and Farrah were ready and had their hands around Wyatt and me the moment I touched the ground. Together, we ran a few feet forward, to get away from the mansion, but I couldn't go much longer. When it seemed safe enough, I folded to my knees and dropped Wyatt on the ground.

We all started coughing. Black spots filled my vision and my head swam. I glanced at the girls and found them not much better than me—after effects of the smoke.

But Farrah still had some sense in her. She summoned her powers and swirled a giant tornado of icy air around us. Somehow, she had her magic draw out the smoke from our lungs and soon we were breathing much better. She did the same with Wyatt. The young wolf made a noise that sounded like a cough, showing signs he was still alive.

Relief flooded Farrah's face, and Luana let out a long sigh.

"Wyatt." I patted his shoulder, trying to wake him up.

He snapped his eyes open.

"Wyatt," Farrah called out, her voice gentle.

His eyes found hers. His expression changed instantly. Wyatt jumped to his paws and snarled at her.

Then he took off.

"Wyatt, wait!" Luana shouted, but it was to no avail.

"I guess he's still under Soren's spell," Farrah muttered.

I glanced at her. It was clear she liked him, maybe even as a good friend, but it hurt her to see him like this as much as it hurt Luana and me. I tried to come up with something to say to her, to make her feel better, but as I opened my mouth, grunts and shouts filtered from the corner of the mansion.

The freaking fight in the backyard. It was still going on.

The three of us rounded the corner and skidded to a halt. Despite the noises, the battle was practically done with most of Zell's warlocks dead. The coven was gone.

Luana's hand wrapped around my upper arm. "You want to help them?"

I shook my head. "There's no point." They had lost, and if we tried to help now, in our current state, we would end up dead too.

As much as I would like to save everyone, I couldn't. My main goal was to battle Soren and he wasn't here right now. To be able to fight him again, I had to go somewhere and rest.

Luana tugged on my arm. "Then we should go."

I nodded and let her guide me out of there.

WITHOUT MANY CHOICES, WE WENT BACK TO LUANA'S HOUSE AT the Dark Vale pack. We took showers, ate a hearty meal, and then we talked while we cleaned up the kitchen. We should probably go to bed and sleep, but our minds were too abuzz with all the wrong turns this cursed day had taken. We needed to clear the twisty path in front of us before we could lay our heads down and allow sleep to come.

"We lost Soren and Isalia," Luana said as she washed the dishes at the sink. "And Wyatt."

Farrah picked up the plate from her and dried it with a towel. "We'll get them."

"How?" I asked as I picked up the plate from Farrah and put it away. "We need a better plan."

"They probably returned to the Chateau of the Curse," Farrah said, handing me a glass. "We could try to storm it now."

Luana shook her head. "We've done that and we failed. I'm sure they took measures and are ready should we try again."

"Right." I nodded. "We need something else."

"How about we just wait?" Farrah asked. "I'm sure they will come for you two at some point."

"Meanwhile, everyone else in their path suffers," I said. "And your people too. Doesn't your brother want you to return?"

She lowered her head, as if she didn't want to acknowledge that. Why? Was she having more problems with her brother?

"I agree." Luana handed the last plate to Farrah and turn off the faucet. "We can't wait for them. Who knows what they will do in the meantime? If we sit and wait, they might go after Thea and Drake before they come to us."

Farrah furrowed. "That would be stupid."

Luana's lips turned up. "I never said they were clever."

But they were freaking clever, maybe not in every way, but they were. Otherwise, they wouldn't have gotten to where they were.

Something about what Farrah said stuck in my head, though. *I'm sure they will come for you too.* Especially if we gave them the proper motivation.

"We'll try our original plan again," I said.

"What do you mean?" Luana asked.

"We'll bring Soren and Isalia out of the Chateau of the Cursed."

Farrah glanced from me, to Luana, and back to me. "How?"

A confident grin spread over my lips. "I'll be the bait."

THE SICK FEELING IN MY STOMACH DIDN'T WANT TO LEAVE ME. It came on after Keeran told me and Farrah that he wanted to use himself as bait to draw Soren to him. Wasn't that similar to our first plan? And yet, something was different now. I could see it in him. And that what made me sick.

I asked him about it, but he said he wasn't sure of the details yet. He would think some more before sharing. And just like that, we went to bed and slept. Despite my exhaustion and sores and aches, and now my worry over Keeran's untold plan, I fell into a deep sleep.

The next morning, Keeran had a quick breakfast and disappeared from the house, saying he was going to work on his plan.

As soon as the front door closed, Farrah turned to me. "Is he all right?"

I shrugged. "I don't know. He won't tell me anything."

"He looks kind of … obsessed."

I nodded. "I think so too."

"So." Farrah put her hands on her hips and looked

around my humble house. "What can we do to pass the time around here?"

"Nothing much." Unless she wanted to go for a swim at the lake, but honestly, I wasn't in the mood for that. I had something else in mind. "I was thinking about training. You know ... I'll probably face Isalia soon and she's still stronger than me."

Farrah looked at me as if I was crazy. "She's not stronger than you."

"Well, so far, I've lost to her one too many times. I would like to change that. So I'm about to train. Want to join me?"

"It's better than standing around here staring at the walls."

I gave her some of my training clothes—stretch pants, tank top, and sneakers—and met her in the backyard. We had training grounds, but I didn't feel like crossing the village to get there. I wanted to stay here, close to my house, where I felt safer, and where Keeran was supposed to meet us once he was done with whatever he was doing.

I deposited a neatly folded stack of crappy T-shirts right outside the back door. Farrah watched me with a curious glint in her eyes. "If I'm to fight Isalia, I have to shift, which means, I'll be naked once I shift back." I gestured to the pile. "And I brought several, in case I rip through some."

"Is that normal? Having dozens of spare clothes?"

I nodded. "It is, but most are just crappy stuff. There's no point in having nice clothes when you know you might have to shift without a second to spare."

"I get it." She glanced down at the clothes I had lent her. "These are not bad, though."

"Well, I did say most." I reached for the hem of my shirt. "Turn around if seeing me naked bothers you."

Farrah smiled. "Oh, if only you knew how the fae court is. Seeing people half naked or even naked is not unusual."

That made me pause. "Then tell me."

Farrah waved me off. "There's nothing to tell. Let's train."

I tried not to let her dismissal get to me, but it did. I had come to consider Farrah a friend, even with our age difference, and it hurt a little bit that she didn't trust me enough to talk about her homeland or her problems.

However, pushing her right now wouldn't do any good. So I let it go—for now—and undressed. A moment later, I shifted.

I let out a short howl, signaling I was ready.

Farrah brought up her hands and five ice soldiers sprouted from the ground in front of her. Each one held a different weapon: a long sword, bow and arrows, axe, twin swords, and one had his hands transformed into big claws.

All right. This wasn't what I had in mind. I thought she would fight me, but I guess she was ready to use all her tricks, including this.

I couldn't blame her. If I had neat spells like this, I would use them all the time.

The soldiers charged, all at once.

My heart raced as I leaped on the sword soldier, knocking his weapon out of his hand and biting his neck. Instantly, the soldier dissolved into snowflakes that melted when they met the ground.

I didn't have time to admire Farrah's work as an arrow landed a millimeter from my paw. I turned to attack the bow and arrow soldier, but the one with the axe jumped on me first. I felt the swoop of the blade half an inch from my back as I ducked under his hit and spun out of the way. I stuck my paws on the ground, forcing myself to turn like a whip, and reached forward, biting the soldier's waist. I pressed hard, sinking my teeth deep, and pulled back, ripping half of his stomach out. The soldier turned into snow and water in an instant.

An arrow zoomed past my muzzle. I snarled at the archer soldier before running at him. But before I could get to him, the twin swords soldier blocked my path, his blades ready. My heart jumped to my throat as I skidded to a stop and turned to my right, to avoid the full strike of his swords, but I couldn't avoid it all. One of the blades swept over my shoulder. I let out a yelp, but when I glanced at myself, there was no blood on my fur. That was impossible.

I didn't have time to mull over that, though, as he turned around and swung his swords right at my head. I pulled back enough to avoid the blow, then jumped on him. I closed my jaw right on his cheek and buried my front paws in his chest, sinking my long nails deep.

The soldier fell with me, but he was gone before he hit the ground, and I had to scurry so as not to land on my face.

I cried in pain as an arrow embedded in my side. I glanced at the protruding arrow, but it melted a moment later, leaving not even a hole behind.

Again, I didn't have time to understand Farrah's powers as another arrow came for me. I barely had time to dodge it before the soldier sent another one at me. I jumped out of the way.

That was it. I had had it with this soldier.

As I expected, the clawed soldier came at me just as I started after the archer, but I wouldn't pause now. I sidestepped the clawed soldier and zigzagged out of the way, running right to the archer.

He knocked another arrow in place, but I was ready. He

let it out and I twisted out of the way. I bent my knees on my next step, gaining some momentum, and jumped on him. I ripped out his throat, and he melted into water on the ground.

A growl sounded behind me.

I turned around and stared as the clawed soldier fell on all fours and turned into a huge ice wolf.

Holy shit, Farrah!

I didn't have time to recover from my shock or even think of my next step as the ice wolf came at me, his big paws shaking the ground with each fall.

The wolf opened his huge mouth, showing off the row of sharp teeth, most as long as my whole paw. He snapped his teeth at me, taunting me.

I ran toward the wolf. Holding my breath, I waited until he was in front of me, his big mouth again open and ready to bite my head off, and ducked under him. I slid underneath him, and using my hind legs, pressed on the ground to stop. With his momentum, the ice wolf kept going a few more steps, but by then it was too late.

I jumped on his back and bit his shoulder, aiming for a thick vein or an artery.

I bit down on the wolf's shoulder twice more, before he was able to throw me off. I landed hard on the grass, right on my side. The air fled from my lungs. I pushed to my feet, but the wolf was already on top of me, pushing me down again. I clawed his mouth with all I had, until he turned his muzzle to the side. That was my opening. I rolled under his head, getting into a better position, and bit his neck from underneath. This time, I used my claws too—I sank them into the sides of the neck and pulled them down, opening gashes across his skin.

The wolf howled and jerked, trying to dislodge me, but I was glued to him like a moth to the flame. I kept maiming him, cutting him, until finally, his legs gave away and he fell over me. His form melted into water—washing over me.

Like a wet duck, I stood and shifted back.

Farrah came forward with a T-shirt. "You did well."

Catching my breath, I put on the T-shirt. "I don't know what to say first. Should I tell you how impressed I am with your powers, or should I yell at you, because what the hell was that?" I took in a sharp inhale, trying to calm down my still racing heart. "Were you trying to kill me?"

"As you saw, you were bitten, scratched, struck by an arrow, and yet you're not hurt."

"But it did hurt." I glanced at my shoulder and my side. There were no wounds, no holes, no blood, not even scratches. "Is that part of your magic?"

"More or less. I just needed to use a little trick, but your mind did the rest. Your body believed it had been hurt, so your mind believed it too." She smiled at me, as if proud of herself. "Want to try something else?"

Despite the desire to slap her, I had to admit that I was impressed with her abilities. She was amazing.

I shook my head. "I want a break." I grabbed a water bottle from beside the shirt stack and sat down on the grass.

Farrah sat down beside me. She looked up at the bright sun, her silver hair shining, then closed her eyes, as if taking the warmth in.

"Tell me about you," I said. "Like, you have ice powers, but you're now enjoying the sun." She lowered her head and looked at me. I was always so startled with the brilliant blue hue of her eyes.

"I'm from the Frost court. I'm used to the cold, and

because of that, visiting the Blaze court was torture, but you see, the summer here is much milder than the weather at the Blaze court. I like summer here. Shame it's already over."

It was the first time she had shared anything about her, and I was surprised. I wanted to keep asking her about the fae realm, but I was afraid I would be allowed only a certain number of questions, so I changed the course of the conversation to something I was even more curious about.

"Is there something going on between Wyatt and you?"

Her eyes widened, probably taken aback with the new direction I was pushing. Then, a frown formed between her delicate brows. "No, it's not like that."

"Are you sure? I always think I sensed something when you two are around each other."

She looked down at the grass at her feet. "I like him, but as a friend."

"And you think he feels the same."

"I hope so."

"Why?"

She turned her eyes to me again, a different gleam in them this time. A gleam that resembled pain. "It isn't that simple."

"Nothing in life is."

"He's a werewolf; I'm a fae. He probably has a mate lined up for him somewhere, a beautiful she-wolf who is just waiting to find him."

"You know, werewolves can mate with other species." I gestured down to myself. "Look at me. I'm mated to Keeran, a warlock."

Farrah shook her head. "It doesn't matter, because even if it came to something like that, I can't. I would die if I ever got together with Wyatt." I stared at her. What did she just say? I opened my mouth to ask her about it, but she was faster. "How about you and Keeran? Is everything okay with you two?"

I wanted to know more about what the hell she meant about dying, but I got the hint. She didn't want to talk about it, and if I pressed the subject, she would just shut me out again. And after she had opened up to me, I wasn't willing to risk that.

"It's okay, I guess." I paused. Now it was my turn to be honest with her, so she would trust me more and do the same in the future. "We just found out we're mates, so things are complicated."

Farrah nodded. "I bet."

I sipped my water. "I'm worried about him."

"About what?"

"The prophecy," I confessed. "I don't know what scares me the most: That Soren will be stronger and kill him, or that he'll win but evil will claim him."

"You really believe in the prophecy?"

I nodded. "I met the witch who made the prophecy. She said her prophecies are never wrong."

"I know it's hard, but try to be optimistic," Farrah said. "I'm sure we can stop him from turning evil or reverse it if it happens."

"That's what I would like to believe."

"And what's stopping you?"

"I guess if we had a plan for reversing the evil beforehand, I would feel better about it, but we don't have time to figure that out now."

Farrah nudged my shoulder with her elbow. "Don't worry. We'll find a way."

I liked the way she said "we." That meant she wanted to

hang out with us after this was done. Didn't she need to go back to her brother and their fae group? Another question I shouldn't ask yet.

Instead, I pushed to my feet. "Let's get back to training. Show me what other cool tricks you have."

With a smile, Farrah stood and faced me. "You asked for it."

We went back to our previous places. I reached for my shirt and—

"You don't need to take your clothes off." It was Keeran. I whipped around and found him marching toward us from the side of the house. "Not yet, at least."

Farrah made an "ew" sound I was sure only I heard.

Stifling a chuckle, I asked, "Where were you?"

"Just around the village." He waved his hand in the general direction of the main square.

"Did you find what you were looking for?" I wished I knew what that was so I could have helped.

"I did." Something like eagerness shone in his eyes. "My plan is ready."

## 20

KEERAN

Eagerness flowed through my veins. I had found it. I had found a freaking solution and I couldn't wait to share it with Luana.

I brought the girls back into the house, and they sat around the dining table with me.

Luana's fingers hammered on the table. "So, tell us."

I knew she was as eager as I was to end this war, but I knew she was nervous too. For me. She was afraid of my outcome—evil or dead.

But I had found another choice.

"My plan is to send a message to Soren to meet me outside the chateau, without his warlocks, at an appointed time."

Farrah tsked. "How are you gonna send him a message?"

"To be honest, I still have to figure that part out, but I'm thinking through magic," I confessed. "Maybe enchant some paper to appear in his hand. Or you can carry the paper through the air using the wind."

Farrah nodded. Apparently, that would work.

"Okay," Luana said, her voice tight. "You lure him out. Great. And then what?"

"I'll get to that," I promised. "I looked around the houses for scraps of metal, more specifically, for cheap jewelry no one would really miss. Then I found a house with a shed in the back with lots of tools—it looked like a small metallurgy shop, really—and began working." I placed my horrible art piece on the table. It wasn't supposed to be pretty; it was just supposed to work.

Farrah leaned over the table. "What's that?"

"An amulet." A crude chain attached to a silver diamond-shaped pendant with a cheap white crystal the size of my thumbnail in the middle. I had found the chain, the pendant, and the crystal separate. I reinforced parts of the chain, and attached the crystal to the pendant, but it seemed sturdy enough. "It's designed as a special prison. My plan is to get close to Soren, but instead of killing him, I'll imprison him here." I would imbue the crystal with magic to hold him there. "This way, I don't need to kill him and I won't turn evil." At least, that was the theory.

"I like that," Farrah said, smiling. "But are you sure this pendant will hold a powerful warlock?"

"Sure? No, but it's worth a try." I picked up the amulet by the chain and stared at the crystal. "What I think will happen is that I will have to keep the magic fresh."

Farrah nodded. "That might work."

I sighed. "The only problem is that this spell will probably take a lot of my power and I'll be vulnerable. I'll have to trap him quickly. Otherwise, it might not work."

"We'll help you with that." Farrah glanced at Luana. "Right?"

I held my breath as I turned my gaze to Luana. She was

quiet, with a slight frown in between her brows, which meant she was holding something in. "Tell me what you're thinking."

"I ..." She pressed her lips tight, as if measuring her words before speaking. That was a first. "I'm worried about this. Yes, it's a nice plan, but like you said, you'll have to get close to him. You know he won't waste a second attacking you. You'll have to defend yourself and cast this trapping spell at the same time. It's too risky."

"I know but—"

"I can't believe I'm the one saying this, since I'm the werewolf with the explosive temper, but we can't be that risky." Her voice grew harder, but the glint in her eyes showed me something else: concern. "We have to come up with a plan we're sure will be infallible."

"You know as well as I do that no plan works exactly as planned."

"All the more reason to think of a better one," she snapped. There was her temper. "Didn't you just say this might work? If something goes wrong, then it just won't work."

"When you put it that way," Farrah whispered.

Luana pointed at her. "See? Even Farrah agrees with me."

"Hey." Farrah raised her hands. "That wasn't what I said."

"Luana ..."

She glared at me. "Don't Luana me. You're telling me you're just gonna stand there while Soren attacks you and you cast a spell that you aren't sure will work. And if it works, you aren't sure how long it'll last. I vote no."

I wanted to be mad at her for not agreeing to this plan, but deep down, I understood why she was against it. Because she was worried about me. She didn't want to lose me, as I didn't want to lose her.

But our lives weren't normal. Our problems were too big to sit back and hope for the best. Even when we defeated Soren and Isalia, I was sure more enemies would show up eventually.

That was the nature of living as a supernatural.

"Luana," I tried again.

She slapped the table and shot to her feet. "No, don't. Don't even try."

Cursing under her breath, Luana marched out of the house, slamming the back door on her way.

What the hell had happened?

I stood to go after her, but Farrah's hand on my arm made me pause.

"Give her some time," she said. "Luana needs some time alone to calm down. After that, you two can talk again."

I groaned. "As if that would change her mind."

Leaning back in her chair, Farrah shrugged. "Who knows? Nothing is impossible."

I stared at the closed door, wishing it was that simple. Wishing Luana calmed down in the next five minutes and came to me. Not to apologize—I didn't want that—but to support me. Despite all her worries, I had already made up my mind. I was going forward with this plan, with or without her.

All I could do was wish she was with me.

---

## 21

I STAYED AWAY ALL DAY, RUNNING IN MY WOLF FORM THROUGH the forest, burning some of the pent-up feelings bottled inside me.

Why did I feel like this? Why did I feel like if Keeran faced Soren that way, he would die? My mate would die.

I stomped my paws on the ground and skidded to a stop by the entrance of a cave in the mountainside, a place I used to come a lot when I was a pup.

Why had I come here?

My paws must have brought me to where I felt comfortable, even if my mind wasn't conscious of it.

Shifting back into my human form—and holding the crystal flower I had brought with me—I walked into the cave.

Once I slammed the back door and walked out the house, I transformed into a wolf and my clothes fell into scraps on the ground, along with the crystal flower that had been in my pocket. I almost ran off, leaving it behind, but at the last second, I came back and bit it, keeping it tight between my teeth.

The cave was dark, but wide, and at the end, a small streak ran through the rocks, bringing in a little light from the outside.

I sat down on a rock jutting out from the ground and dipped my toes in the water. I glanced at the crystal flower.

"Aren't you magical? Aren't you supposed to protect me or whatever? Then do something."

I had meant for it to protect Keeran while he went through with his plan, or give me some temporary magical powers so I could protect him. Instead, the flower glowed, bathing the cave in a bright red light.

I closed my eyes against the brightness and an image flashed in my mind.

A prosperous and vast land, encompassing the Dark Vale land and the land around it. Sturdy houses, clean streets, lots of plants and woods, and a wide square where a beautiful couple stood atop of an intricate wooden platform, holding a baby.

Me.

I just knew deep in my core that baby was me.

The image changed. I was now a little girl of maybe two or three, playing in the backyard of my house, while my mother worked in the garden. In his wolf form, my father jumped over the fence and came to stand beside me. I reached for him, so, so little beside him, but he lowered his big head and rested his forehead against mine. Despite the fact that wolfs could only communicate when shifted, I could hear his words in my mind as clear as day.

*I'm proud of you, Luana. When you grow up, you'll be a great alpha to our people.*

The picture changed again.

Noises woke me up from my sleep. Curious, I padded out

of my bedroom, and saw the most horrific scene: my parents on their bedroom floor, and blood everywhere.

A scream caught in my throat and I trembled as I backed away.

Then a wolf walked out of the room.

She shifted into her human form.

Isalia.

I gasped and tried opening my eyes to end this crazy dream, but I couldn't. I was trapped in these lost memories, watching as Isalia smiled at me, a wicked grin that sent a chill down my spine.

She walked toward me.

She would kill me.

I knew it.

But as she lifted her arm and shifted it into a claw, two other wolves jumped her. She shifted and fought them.

The vision flashed, changing again.

The couple now ran from the house, carrying me in their arms. Behind us, we could hear shouts and screams as people found their beloved leaders killed. Had this couple killed Isalia? They couldn't have, or she wouldn't torment my life even now. No, they must have been able to fight her off and take me away.

They should have killed her.

The memory changed.

The couple hid in the woods with me. The woman knelt in front of me.

"Your new name is Luana and we're your parents now, okay?" she said, her big brown eyes worried, but warm. "If anyone asks, we found you lost in the forest, okay? Can you do that?"

I didn't answer. I was too scared, in shock.

The man put a heavy hand on my small shoulder. "Don't worry. We won't hurt you. We're trying to save you. You can trust us. We'll always protect you."

The image changed again.

I was a little older now, living in the cabin I had run from with my foster parents, but for some reason, I didn't remember they weren't my real parents. I didn't remember anything from the past.

The young me walked out of her bedroom and found her parents whispering in the kitchen.

"We should tell her," my mother said. "It's time."

"No, it's not time," my father argued. "If we want her to live, it'll never be time. If she ever finds out, that she-wolf will kill her too."

At the time, I had no idea what they were talking about, but I knew who they were talking about. Isalia. Our pack, Dark Vale, was small, said to have been separated from a bigger pack a few years back, but no one was allowed to talk about it. Talking about the past was forbidden by the alpha, Ulric. And Isalia had showed up in our pack and become the alpha's mate.

"But she knows," my mother whispered. "She must have come to kill her."

My father shook his head. "Not if she doesn't remember. If you think about it, it's a blessing she doesn't remember."

"But what about us?"

My memory changed once more.

I was still a little pup, but now I watched over the bodies of my parents as they were lowered into their graves. Isalia and Ulric stood on the other side of the graves. Ulric seemed focused on the burial rituals, but Isalia had her eyes on me the entire time.

My eyes snapped open.

I gasped and slid to the ground, my breathing hard, my heart hurting against my rib cage. I pressed a hand over my chest and tried to calm down.

How could I calm down after all I saw? All I remembered?

Before Dark Vale, I was the princess of a powerful wolf pack. But for some reason, Isalia sneaked into my house and killed my parents. She was about to kill me when those two wolves stopped her. They took me away before Isalia could get rid of me. Because of the death of my parents, the short-tempered wolves fell into chaos and the pack divided. The original pack was no more, and stronger wolves proclaimed being the alphas of the new, smaller packs.

The couple who saved me ended up under Ulric, the alpha of the Dark Vale. I was so little, no one realized I was the lost princess, and no one questioned how the couple showed up with a daughter. I thought now that they were so worried about rebuilding and keeping an eye on the other packs, in case of attacks, that no one paid attention to me.

But then Isalia showed up. She knew exactly where I was and who I was. I bet she tried to kill me again, but once she realized I didn't remember anything, she left me alone.

And by some crazy fate, she became Ulric's mate. She was close enough to keep an eye on me, and she now had what I thought she wanted: power. She wasn't the alpha, but she was the mate of one. Now, looking back, I wondered if she didn't order him around behind our backs, making her the alpha of the alpha, and thus the owner of the entire Dark Vale.

But something must have happened, because she killed my foster parents too. I was sure of it. And later, when I was older, she had Ulric sent me on that suicide mission to DuMoir Castle.

Little did she know, I would come back from that, kill Ulric, and become alpha.

In the end, I had become the alpha.

I stared at the rose as the red glow lessened.

Incredible. The magic in the flower Keeran had created for me was incredible. It really had protected me and guided me, as Almae said it would.

My legs shaking, I pushed to my feet and inhaled deeply.

With invisible hands, I picked up the ball of turmoil stirring inside me and locked it away. What I had learned, what I had remembered, was a bomb I couldn't let out. I was born to be the pack leader, and Isalia wouldn't take that away from me. But it wasn't time to use this bomb yet. Regardless, I felt confident. I felt sure.

I stopped shaking; my breathing slowed down.

Head high, I walked out of the cave.

---

I HEARD HIS FRANTIC BREATHING, HIS FAST HEARTBEAT, AND HIS heavy footfall as he paced side to side before I saw him.

When I appeared in the backyard as the sun was coming down, Keeran stilled and stared at me.

"Luana!" He rushed to me. "Where have you been?"

I placed the crystal rose on the grass and shifted into my human form. Keeran took off his shirt and pulled it over my head.

"Thanks," I whispered.

He grabbed my shoulders, holding me tight as if he was afraid I would run away again. "I was worried."

"I know." I nodded. "I'm sorry."

He shook his head and embraced me. "It's okay. I'm just glad you're back."

I wound my arms around his back and rested my head on his chest. This right here felt like home. Keeran with his strong arms, musky scent, and steady heartbeat was my home.

The new things I learned pressed on my chest. I had so much to tell him, but for some reason, the words wouldn't come out. It wasn't because I wanted to hide the truth about my past from him, but because I was tired and I was still processing it.

And he was anxious to work on his plan; I didn't want to steal this moment from him.

I pulled back a little, so I could look up at him. "Let's do it."

A frown adorned his forehead. "What?"

"Your plan," I said. "I'm sorry I overreacted. I think my head wasn't in the right place. But I've thought about it and I support you. I believe in you."

He arched an eyebrow at me. "Really?"

I nodded, rubbing my chin on his chest. "Really. Let's go kick some ass."

It was time.

Luana, Farrah, and I waited in the clearing a couple of miles behind the Chateau of the Cursed. I had sent the magical message to Soren hours earlier, telling him when and where to meet me.

And to come alone.

A few minutes before the appointed time, Farrah nodded at Luana and me, and went to the trees to hide. She was instructed not to act or help me, unless more warlocks or werewolves showed up. Then, she was free to let her magic out and kill everyone if she could.

Deep in my core, I doubted Soren would come alone. But I hoped he would. I hoped, because only then would this battle would be fair, and only then could I rid the world of this evil.

The minutes passed, and Soren still didn't show up. I was starting to doubt he ever got my message in the first place.

To distract me, Luana leaned into me, her head on my shoulder.

"I have something to tell you," she said. I stilled. The last time she said that, she told me I was her mate. Which was great, but could there be more to this? She pulled out the crystal rose from her pocket. "The rose's magic showed me something."

And then she told me a crazy story about her parents being the alphas of a large wolf pack, and her being raised to take over one day. But then Isalia killed her parents. I stared at her in horror as she told me the entire story.

I lifted a finger, needing a moment. "Wait, wait. You're saying Isalia killed both your biological and your foster parents?" She nodded, looking extremely calm for a cranky werewolf. "H-how ...?" I didn't even know what to say to her.

She stared at the rose. "This rose helped me escape from the warlocks before, and it showed me memories I had forgotten. And it's all because of the magic you put in it."

"All I had meant to do was to create something pretty for you, not imbued it with magic." I kissed the top of her head. "But I'm glad it happened. Otherwise, you wouldn't know about your past. What are you going to do?"

She shook her head. "We'll talk about that later. Right now, you should focus on your fight." She looked up at me, a soft smile in her lips. "I believe in you, Keeran. I know you're more powerful than you think you are. If you fight today with love in your heart, for love, you'll win."

Her words sounded so sure, so strong.

I reached to her and cupped her neck, pulling her to me. "I love you," I whispered, before leaning into her and kissing her. She clutched my arms and held me tight as she opened her mouth to me and let me savor her.

I had to keep her in my mind, in my heart. Because if I

didn't think of Luana, the terrible images of when rage took over me and I killed those warlocks filled my head, and despair clawed its way through my core.

No, I had to be strong. For Luana. For us.

"They are here," Luana whispered against my lips.

We broke apart and straightened.

A moment later, Soren walked into the clearing.

Followed by Isalia.

After all Luana had told me, I felt the urge to charge at Isalia and kill her myself. I bet she would never expect it from me, not so suddenly. But I knew Luana had to do that on her own, just as I had to deal with my dear father on my own.

"They came alone?" I asked Luana in a low voice.

By now she should have been able to hear if there were warlocks and werewolves hiding in the forest.

She dipped her chin once. "Yes."

Soren and Isalia halted a few yards from us.

"I received your message," Soren said, his tone casual. He glanced around, seeming totally bored. "Have you brought me here for a fight?"

"That's right," I said.

"Before you two start." Luana took a step forward. "I would like to ask Isalia to follow me."

Isalia's brows cocked up. "Are you going to challenge me too?"

Luana's hands closed into fists. I could see she was trying to be civil, at least for now. "It'll depend on what you say after our little talk."

A wicked smile graced Isalia's lips. "A talk. All right. I want to know what you want to talk about." She waved her fingers at Soren. "See you soon, dear."

Luana glanced at me, then walked out of the clearing with Isalia.

With big gestures and a wave of his arms, Soren took off his cloak and threw it aside. "Are you ready?"

I took off my cloak and folded my sleeves. "More than you think."

## 23

LUANA

I GUIDED ISALIA TO ANOTHER, SMALLER CLEARING, NOT FAR from where Keeran and Soren were. As much as I wanted to be there for him, I knew it was best if I didn't see his fight—because I didn't want to risk interfering without meaning to, and I thought he could get distracted by trying to keep tabs on me.

I stopped in the center of the clearing and turned to Isalia. She still had her evil witch smile stamped on her face. I was dying to kill here right now, right here—and I planned on doing just that—but first I needed answers. I needed to make sure my memories were right.

"So." She glanced around at the clearing as if it was much different than the others. "Are we battling here?"

"I know what you did," I told her, going straight to the point. "I know you killed my parents, thus destroying my pack."

Her wicked smile only widened. "I thought you couldn't remember the past."

"I remembered." I felt the wolf in me asking for release. I

wanted to shift and kill her so bad. "Why? Tell me why you did it?"

She snarled at me. "I don't owe you any answers."

"But you do. You killed all four of my parents and you expect me to let it go?"

She seemed to consider it for a moment. "My parents were lone wolves who were killed by wolves from your pack."

I frowned. "There must have been a reason." I had to believe there was. Wolves didn't go around killing each other. No one did. Unless there was a big reason.

"A reason? We got too close to your pack territory and your guards thought we were there to infiltrate or spy." She let out a hollow chuckle. "No matter how much my parents argued that we were just passing by, the guards didn't believe them. They were killed in front of my eyes. I was left alone in the forest, barely a teenager, to fend for myself." She bared her teeth at me. "I promised that when I was strong enough, I would come back to kill the leaders who had allowed that to happen, and everyone else in my path. And if I happen to inherit the pack from the alpha, so be it."

"But you didn't kill me," I whispered.

"No, that ridiculous couple who worked at the main house whisked you away before I could finish you. And I couldn't—"

"Become alpha," I whispered. What did it mean? That I was still alpha of my father's pack? But the pack didn't exist anymore. It was impossible.

She nodded. "Thankfully, nobody else saw me that night and I was able to go after you later at the Dark Vale pack. Imagine my surprise when I got there and became the true mate of their alpha. I might not have been alpha, but I got the power and stability I wanted."

"Power and stability. Wasn't that enough? You had to kill my foster parents?"

"They knew too much. And as you grew older, you grew stronger. I knew they would tell you about your past, and you would be able to not only reclaim the Dark Vale pack, but all of the others that had been created from its fall."

"So you killed them."

"I did. I wanted to kill you too, but I was sure you didn't remember anything." She let out a long breath. "But you kept growing right in front of my eyes, and I just knew you would be able to defeat us all someday. So, I made Ulric send you on that suicide mission."

Rage and frustration and pain swam in my core. I wanted to kill her so, so bad, but I was afraid that if I attacked her here and now, my fury would make me sloppy and I would lose again. I couldn't lose to her ever again. So, I pushed those feelings back and focused on the amusing part of her game. "Too shocked I survived that too?"

She snorted. "It seems like you really don't want to die."

Until recently, I didn't have a purpose in my life. I was simply afraid of death, like everyone else. But now it was different. I had been someone with a fate, with a destiny, and I could be that someone again. I could take my rightful place, unite the wolf packs, and create a peaceful and fair world for the werewolves.

I clenched my fists as the rage took over all of my other feelings. This was it. I was going to kill her right now. "Enough chitchat," I snarled. "Time for our challenge."

Isalia shook her head. "I'm sorry to disappoint you, but I won't be fighting today."

What the hell? "Why not?"

She placed a hand over her stomach. "You wouldn't kill a pregnant wolf, would you?"

A gasp rose in my throat and my jaw dropped. She … what? I glanced at her stomach. She was pregnant? Was that true? I focused on my hearing, blocking everything else, but the both of us in the clearing. No, the three of us. Sure enough, a strong, fast heartbeat inside her stomach.

I slapped my mouth with my hand. She was pregnant. With Soren's baby. Keeran's half-sibling.

Holy shit.

A child who would be half-warlock, half-werewolf—a powerful combination. Being raised by both Soren and Isalia, this child would not only be powerful, but evil.

Maybe the best thing for this child was to not be born at all.

I shook my head. What the hell was I thinking? The child wasn't the one to blame here, and if she was raised right, she would be able to use her powers for good.

I inhaled deeply, calming my rage and shock. "We'll honor the rules of the pack and we won't duel until after the baby is born."

Isalia nodded. "Agreed."

It took everything in me not to say "screw this" and kill her anyway, but I couldn't. My morals and the rules of the pack were clear: I wouldn't harm an unborn baby or a young pup. We would wait until after the birth to duel.

Hopefully, Keeran would have dealt with Soren by then, and we would have one last enemy to take care of.

A scream cut through the clearing, and I turned my head in its direction, my heart skipping a beat. "Keeran."

---

## 24

KEERAN

As I expected, Soren attacked me half a second after the duel started.

I cast a thick shield in front of me and channeled my power. My magic swelled in my veins. It was hard to control, but I sent most of it to the amulet, to start the spell.

Several of Soren's strikes hit the shield, shaking it and sending a ripple of power and resistance through me.

I gritted my teeth, sending more power to the shield while still feeding the amulet. I felt my core being torn in two. If I had to keep this up for too long, I would faint from exhaustion.

Soren threw a black bolt that finally broke the shield.

I felt it inside me and my knees wobbled.

I had to distract him.

Without much choice, I sent a big wave of red magic at him. Hopefully, it would keep him busy for a few seconds— or however long I needed to make this amulet work. As much as I wanted to have prepared beforehand, I couldn't. I had come up with the spell I was using, and it required the presence of the person I would imprison in it.

Once the wave left my hands, I focused on the amulet and infused it with my power.

But Soren was too freaking powerful. He parted the wave, and it faded away to his side, as if it was made of a gentle breeze.

Meanwhile, my magic was draining and I was weakening.

I tried again, only this time, I threw several dart-like strikes at him, coming from all directions and with different timing. A second after I cast the spell, I turned to the amulet and projected my power into it.

Without any effort, Soren raised his hands and stopped all the darts in midair.

I was so shocked, I let go of my magic and the amulet powered down.

I was back at zero.

A wicked grin stretched over Soren's lips as he turned the darts around and threw them at me.

Panic gripped my chest as I scurried to call on my now weak magic and created a shield in front of me. The shield came up, but it flickered with the first darts and was gone the next second.

A rain of darts hit me on the chest and arms. Pain spread through my muscles, and a scream burst from my throat.

Laughing as if I had told him a joke, Soren strolled toward me. "What are you playing at here? I can feel you're not using your entire power against me. Why?"

The pain ricocheting through my body lessened enough for me to push up to my feet. "Why? Are you tired of dueling already?"

He laughed again. "My dear son, I love dueling. It's fun."

I snorted. "Only you would think dueling is fun."

"Of course it is fun. Or you think coming here and killing you two seconds later is fun? Because I could do that, you know. I could kill you right here, right now."

"Then why don't you?" I shouldn't have asked that, but I couldn't stop the words from rushing past my lips.

"Well, if you insist." Black flames enveloped his arms as he advanced on me.

I summoned my power, but I was hurting too much and my focus was scattered. Only a little magic answered.

I was freaking doomed.

I opened my mouth to tell him some joke, to tease him and gain some time while I recovered enough to call more of my magic, when Luana burst into the clearing in her wolf form.

A second later, Isalia appeared at the edge of the trees. Wyatt, in his wolf form, stood by her side.

Wait. What had happened? When had Wyatt shown up? Why weren't Luana and Isalia fighting? Why wasn't Isalia dead?

But before I could organize my thoughts and ask anything, another strike zoomed my way.

I barely had time to jump out of the way.

Meanwhile, Luana ran to Soren.

He threw his magic at her, but she leaped out of the way, avoiding all the hits, and advancing on him.

When Soren realized he wouldn't stop her so easily, it was already too late. With one last jump, Luana landed on Soren and bit down on his shoulder.

A scream echoed through the night.

I held on to the amulet and called my power. I focused on

it, hard and deep, hoping that even though I was tired and hurt and weak, it was enough.

In the back of my mind, I wondered why Isalia wasn't attacking, why she wasn't protecting Soren and fighting against us, but I ignored those thoughts as much as I could while I charged the amulet.

I begged the moon, the stars, the old gods, even Bagatha, the old queen of all witches, to give me enough strength, to help me once more. The magic burned through my veins as it traveled down my arms, to my fingertips, and into the amulet.

Finally, after what felt like an eternity, the amulet thrummed in my palm.

It was full. It was ready.

Without wasting a second, I rushed to where Luana and Soren brawled. He tried getting rid of her with magic, but she had bitten his hands, which probably made casting magic a little more challenging.

I knelt beside them and placed my free hand over Soren's chest. I poked at the magic and the spell started instantly.

"What are you doing?" Soren shouted, his bugged eyes on the amulet. "What's that?"

Luana clamped her teeth on his shoulder again. Throwing his head back, Soren screamed, then his body relaxed, as if he didn't have much fight inside him anymore.

Losing to the spell, Soren's body started shimmering. He was weakening fast. He couldn't fight this now even if he wanted to.

Sensing it was almost done, Luana retreated a couple of steps.

"Goodbye, father," I whispered.

Soren jerked one last time before his entire body became

a puff of gray smoke. As if hit by a draft of wind, the smoke swirled into the amulet, filing the stone in the center.

Silence fell on the clearing.

It was done.

Soren was gone, imprisoned inside the amulet.

In her human form, Luana knelt beside me. "You did it. You defeated your father."

I stared at her, still dumbfounded. I had hoped this spell would freaking work, but to be honest, a sliver of doubt had plagued me since I first came up with the idea. I turned my gaze to the amulet. I still couldn't believe I had done it.

A thought popped in my mind and I shot to my feet.

"Isalia," I said, looking at the werewolf at the edge of the trees.

Her skin was paler than usual, and her eyes were bugged, as if she too couldn't believe what I had done.

Beside her, Wyatt growled at us.

I clenched my fists and channeled my magic. I didn't care that Luana had to kill Isalia to become alpha of her pack. I could injure her at least once. That should help with Luana's duel.

Although, to my surprise, Luana held my arms. "No, don't attack her."

My magic faded away. "What? Why not?"

"I'll explain later," she said, her voice low.

"Wyatt," Isalia said. "Kill them."

The young wolf let out a growl before rushing us.

I called my magic, intent on stunning him, not killing him.

But before I could do anything, Farrah jumped out of her hideout. "Don't hurt him!" she said, her hands out. Ice rose from the ground as if it were vines, and grew around Wyatt's paws, trapping him.

When I glanced at Isalia, I found her spot empty. The coward she-wolf had fled.

Slowly, Farrah approached Wyatt.

He growled at her.

"I trapped Soren." I squeezed the amulet in my hand. "Shouldn't the spell have broken by now?"

Eyes on Wyatt, Farrah shook her head. "He's trapped in there." She absently pointed to me, indicating the amulet. "He's not dead, so no, his spell wasn't broken."

"What do we do now?" Luana had found my cloak on the ground and covered herself with it. "We can't leave him like this."

Farrah turned her blue eyes to me. "Remember when we got out of the burning manor, and I used my magic to flush out the smoke from our lungs?" Luana and I nodded. "I can guide your magic, Keeran, inside Wyatt's body like that. This way, we should be able to find where this spell is hiding. We can grab it and expel it from his body."

I frowned. "How do you know that will work?"

"I don't," Farrah admitted. "But we have to try."

The agony was stamped on her face, in the hard set of her shoulders, in her voice. We all knew she cared about Wyatt, and Wyatt cared about her. If it was Luana like that, I would do anything, I would try anything to save her.

I stepped closer. "Tell me what to do."

"Just ... cast a bolt of your purest magic," she said. "I'll guide it."

"And then what?"

"I'm pretty sure you'll know what to do once we get there."

Hoping she was right, I closed my eyes and summoned my magic while thinking of good things—Luana, our love, her smile, my magic, my friends—that was the only way I knew how to summon pure magic.

I opened my eyes to a bolt of bright red floating over my palm.

With her icy breeze, Farrah took the bolt. It dissipated in her wind, becoming red air, and swirled into Wyatt's mouth. The young wolf jerked against the ice, growled and snapped his teeth at us, but it seemed that unless Farrah allowed him to, he wasn't getting off that ice today.

I felt my magic rummaging inside Wyatt—every few seconds, the young wolf gasped and coughed, probably from the air traveling within—going from corner to corner, as if searching for a hidden treasure.

Not a treasure.

A curse.

Tucked right underneath his brain was a cloud of dark magic. I imagined my magic becoming like a claw and taking that dark magic, molding it into a tight ball, one I could squeeze into my hand tight, where I wouldn't lose any particles.

Sensing I was ready, Farrah sent another thin wave of air in, and my magic moved with it. I felt as it traveled up Wyatt's throat, past his tongue, and out of his mouth.

I opened my hand, as if I had really been holding to the spell, and let it go.

Red and dark smoke floated in front of us, dissipating into the night air.

Trembling, Wyatt shifted from wolf to human. His muscles visibly jerked as his body folded into itself. Farrah let go of her magic, pulling the ice down and taking Wyatt with it. Finally, Wyatt lay on the grass and the ice was gone.

Luana brought Soren's forgotten cloak and covered Wyatt's quavering body.

"Wyatt?" she called, her voice holding an apprehensive tone. "Are you okay? Are you *you* again?"

Letting out a long breath, Wyatt clutched to the cloak. "I'm me," he said, his voice as weak as he looked.

Luana hooked her hand under his elbow and helped him sit up. "Are you okay?"

He kept his head down, but he nodded.

Farrah stood a few steps to the side, her eyes fixed on him, her body tense. I couldn't imagine what was going through her mind right now.

I couldn't imagine what was going through Wyatt's.

I tried putting myself in his shoes and understand what was going through his mind. He had been believed dead, and because of that, Soren spelled him to become a wild wolf, practically a hunting dog. At Soren's command, Wyatt had maimed and killed.

He had tried hurting us.

From the way he seemed to shrink into himself, I bet he remembered everything. Every little dark and terrible thing he did.

Rage coiled in my core.

I clenched my fists. "We need to end this once and for all. Farrah, take care of Wyatt. Luana and I will go after Isalia." I started moving.

Luana put her hands in my chest, stopping me. "We can't."

I frowned at her. "What? Why?"

She sighed. "Isalia is pregnant."

"What?" Farrah practically shrieked. She took a step forward, but stopped herself again.

It took me a moment to grasp what Luana was saying. Isalia was pregnant. Probably by Soren. My father. Which meant ...

"One of the pack rules is that we can't duel expectant wolves," Luana continued. "We'll have to wait until the pup is born."

"Which should be?" Farrah prompted.

"In about three months," Luana said. "And before any of you protest, I'm already warning you: I won't go against a pack rule. I have to prove I'm good enough to be alpha again. If I start breaking pack rules, I'll be doing exactly the opposite."

"Sounds fair," Farrah said.

"Meanwhile, we should rest." Luana tugged Wyatt's arm, and together, the two of them stood. She glanced at me. "Right?"

I shook my head, sending the troublesome thoughts in my mind scattering. "Right. Let's go."

I took Wyatt's other side and we started our trek back to Luana's cabin at the Dark Vale pack. Farrah walked a few feet behind us.

On the way, I tried keeping my mind clear of the latest news, but something else caught my attention. The amulet, which I had hung around my neck, was alive. I could feel my father stirring inside it, his power and evil rubbing against my skin.

Carrying my father inside an amulet would be harder than I thought.

**25**

———————

LUANA

It had been one long and emotionally draining day. By the time, Keeran and I made it to my bedroom, I was ready to lie down and sleep for ten days.

When we left the clearing and came back to my house, Keeran and I had to half-carry Wyatt out. He didn't say much on the way, just that we should leave him and move on.

I had the idea that he was ashamed or struggling with what he had done while under Soren's and Isalia's control, and now he could barely face us without wanting to hide.

But I wouldn't let him hide. I could give him some space after we made sure he was well and had some of his strength back, but I wouldn't let him run. He was part of my pack, even if it was just the two of us. He was family, and I had to take care of him.

Once home, we cleaned up, made sure everyone's wounds were tended to, and ate a quiet dinner—except for the part when we talked about Isalia's pregnancy and the pack's rules. It wasn't only Dark Vale's rules. Most wolf packs didn't attack pregnant wolves or pups. It was an honor thing. Gladly, Keeran and Farrah seemed to understand and respect it.

After that, Wyatt insisted on staying somewhere else, so I let him move to the house next door. He wanted to be alone, but Farrah wouldn't let him. After some argument, she went with him.

At least, I knew I could count on her when it came to Wyatt.

Exhausted, I threw myself on the bed. "I'm done with this day."

Chuckling, Keeran crawled over me. "Really? I had hopes we would have energy for something else before we slept."

I cocked an eyebrow at him. After all we had been through, I was certain we would crash and hibernate for a week. Although, I had to admit, I had been worried about how he would react to defeating and imprisoning his father.

I was glad to see he was acting normal.

"What do you have in mind?" I asked, teasing.

With a sly smile, Keeran took off the chain with the amulet and placed it inside the drawer of the nightstand. "I'll show you," he said, before crashing into me.

His mouth ravished mine while his hands slipped down my body. His lips, his touch, his weight over me ... I loved it all. I could barely contain my feelings in my chest. I cried out when his fingers worshipped me, and I practically cried of happiness and completion once Keeran slipped inside me.

This, us ... there was nothing like it, and there would never be.

He was mine, and I was his, and it wasn't only because of the mating bond.

It was because we chose each other.

THERE WAS NOTHING BETTER THAN BEING IN KEERAN'S ARMS. After we defeated Isalia and I reclaimed my pack, things would be perfect.

I buried my face in his neck, and his arms tightened around my back. "What is it?" he asked. "I can see something is bothering you."

"Not bothering," I said, my mouth brushing against his skin. "Just a little shaken by Isalia's pregnancy." I pulled back and stared at his eyes. "I don't know if you realized but that child is—"

"My half-brother or sister." He nodded. "I did the math."

"I'm starting to wonder if I'll be brave enough to kill Isalia," I confessed, my voice low.

"Why wouldn't you?"

"Because she's the mother of your half-sibling. Would I be a good alpha if I killed the mother of an innocent baby?"

Keeran shook his head. "You can't think like that. There are too many evil people in the world, and if we stopped killing or imprisoning them, serving justice, just because they had kids, we would only be adding to the chaos and allowing the world to fall into their evil hands."

When he put it that way ...

It was still hard to accept I would have to orphan a child.

I let out a long breath and laid my head back into his neck. "We have about three months until then. Hopefully, I won't have any doubts about that when the time comes."

Keeran kissed the top of my head. "I'm sure you'll know what to do."

I smiled, happy for his trust in me.

Now, I had to trust him.

I pulled back again. "How are you?"

He frowned. "What do you mean?"

"I can see the amulet is taking a lot of energy from you. How are you feeling about that?"

"I'm okay, I think." He glanced at the nightstand, where the amulet was stored. "I just wonder if this is enough to stop the prophecy, or if it will fulfill it." He paused. "Did I find a way of defeating Soren, or is this a way to just put it off?"

I pressed a hand over his heart, the *thump thump* pressing against my palm. "Even if it doesn't hold him for long, you can always let him out and finish him."

He sighed. "I would rather not kill him. Not only because of the whole I'm-going-to-turn-evil thing, but because I'm tired of killing."

"And he's your father. I can't imagine having to kill your own father."

He nodded. "That too." Keeran's brows curled down. "You know what Zell told me about the prophecy? That it was my mother who made it. That was her witchy power."

I sat up in bed, my eyes wide. "Keeran!"

He sat up beside me, startled. "What happened?"

I clutched his shoulders. "I know your mother!"

"W-what?"

"The witch who saved me and took me to Unity—she was the one who made your prophecy. She's your mother." Although she had been using a different name, I thought maybe she had changed it once she started running from Soren.

Keeran's eyes widened. "Are you sure?"

I nodded, suddenly eager with our discovery. "Almae is Acalla, your mother."

"That's ..." He shook his head.

"That's great!" I smiled. "I can take you to her. You can finally meet your mother."

Keeran frowned. "What about the prophecy about Isalia destroying Unity?"

That made me pause. "Well, Isalia will be busy for a while. She won't attack us or anyone else for the next three months. We can go to Unity so you can meet your mother, and we can leave a few days later, to make sure the place stays hidden."

He thought about it for a minute, then a smile spread over his lips. "All right. It's decided. We'll go to Unity."

***

READ THE NEXT INSTALLMENT IN KEERAN'S AND LUANA'S STORY with *The Crystal Rose*, book 6 of the Rite World.

# THANK YOU

Thank you for reading *The Wolf Consort*!

Reviews are very important for authors. If you liked my book, please consider leaving a review on your favorite vendor and/or on goodreads, please!

Grab the next book in the series, *The Crystal Rose*.

Don't forget to sign up for my Newsletter to find out about new releases, cover reveals, giveaways, and more!

If you want to see exclusive teasers, help me decide on covers, read excerpts, talk about books, etc, join my reader group on Facebook: Juliana's Club!

# ABOUT THE AUTHOR

While USA Today Bestselling Author Juliana Haygert dreams of being Wonder Woman, Buffy, or a blood elf shadow priest, she settles for the less exciting—but equally gratifying—life as a wife, a mother, and an author. She resides in North Carolina and spends her days writing about kick-ass heroines and the heroes who drive them crazy.

Subscribe to her mailing list to receive emails of announcement, events, and other fun stuff related to her writing and her books: www.bit.ly/JuHNL

*For more information:*
www.julianahaygert.com

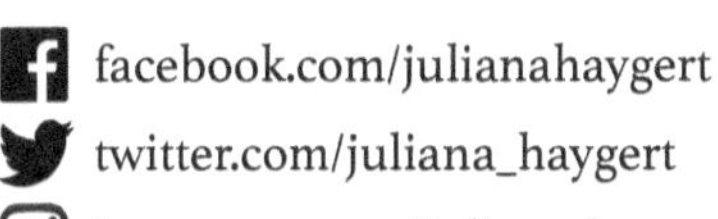

facebook.com/julianahaygert

twitter.com/juliana_haygert

instagram.com/juliana.haygert

# ALSO BY JULIANA HAYGERT

To find links and more info, go to:

www.julianahaygert.com/books/

*Free*

Into the Darkest Fire

Tested

*Rite World: Blackthorn Hunters Academy*

The Demon Kiss (Book 1)

The Hunter Secret (Book 2)

The Soul Bond (Book 3)

The Shadow Trials (Book 4)

The Infernal Curse (Book 5)

*Rite World*

The Vampire Heir (Book 1)

The Witch Queen (Book 2)

The Immortal Vow (Book 3)

The Warlock Lord (Book 4)

The Wolf Consort (Book 5)

The Crystal Rose (Book 6)

The Wolf Forsaken (Book 7)

The Fae Bound (Book 8)

The Blood Pact (Book 9)

*The Fire Heart Chronicles*

Heart Seeker (Book 1)

Flame Caster (Book 2)

Sorrow Bringer (Book 3)

Earth Shaker (Novella)

Soul Wanderer (Book 4)

Fate Summoner (Book 5)

War Maiden (Book 6)

*The Everlast Series*

Destiny Gift (Book 1)

Soul Oath (Book 2)

Cup of Life (Book 3)

Everlasting Circle (Book 4)

*Willow Harbor Series*

Hunter's Revenge (Book 3)

Siren's Song (Book 5)

*Breaking Series*

Breaking Free (Book 1)

Breaking Away (Book 2)

Breaking Through (Book 3)

Breaking Down (Book 4)